RAVENS IN THE *Rain*

A Noir Love Story

CHRISTIE SANTO
& JEFF SANTO

Print ISBN: 978-1-09836-967-5
eBook ISBN: 978-1-09836-968-2

PREFACE

This story is born of our love for film noir. Beyond our visual fascinations for the genre, the intense heavy contrast lighting with Venetian blinds, we're fond of its tropes: the femme fatale and the detective, or the woman with a past and the man with no future. Usually, the protagonist is beaten down by society and lives cynically within its underbelly. We thought that's a lot like relationships today. People are cynical about love but keep mucking around in the dirt anyway. We asked each other, can love grow from such a dark place, where everyone is playing an angle and hope is hard to come by?

So we wrote the screenplay for our neo-noir, *Ravens In The Rain: A Noir Love Story.* Then the Covid-19 pandemic happened, and the world paused. Human interaction became strained; anxiety and homelessness were on the rise. Mentally and emotionally, relationships were tested. For us, it sounded a lot like our story, *Ravens In The Rain.* We knew that a book would allow for a deeper dive into our characters, and we always wanted to write a novel, so that's what we did. Deciding it would take place in 2019 before the pandemic hit when divisions in the United States were rapidly increasing and opportunity lacking. We spent our evenings with

Eddie Mueller on TCM, watching his Noir Alley and our days typing away on our keyboards together like dueling pianos. The result is what you're about to read.

Hope you enjoy.

CHAPTER ONE

In a time where true love is as rare as a thousand dollar bill, and the wealth gap has distanced so many from reality, people have become desperate for any form of a leg-up that they are willing to sacrifice their morals for a sliver of an advantage. Even daring to use love as a currency, they come here, to the Ellis Island Casino, where ominous clouds hang overhead; and its brightly lit neon sign beckons the tired and huddled masses yearning to be lucky.

A beaten white sedan rattles into the lot and parks upfront, its rims blackened from years of neglect. The engine knocks closer to its last breath before going silent. The driver's door opens. Out steps high heels and legs to die for, a striking contrast to the vehicle they stepped out from; *wham* goes the car door.

Her heels strut with purpose toward the candy-stripe awning, win or lose, she'll get what she needs one way or another, and stepping inside, she looks out at the black and grey patchwork flooring. This is no yellow brick road, and she is no Dorothy. She knows this is precisely the sort of place a girl like her belongs, an off-strip casino; it fits the offbeat road she's traveled to get here. She struts past tennis shoes, flip flops, and trash that's missed the bin, but no one cares, to a corral of low-minimum blackjack tables. That's when he sees her, from the craps table, watching with his bluish-grey marbles as he strokes his face, concealing his forbidding pockmarks. There is an elegance about her that sets her apart and draws him in. His sturdy shoulders come to attention as he wonders if her sparkle is what he needs to lift him from his darkness.

Scanning for a table to play, she spots a hundred dollar bill laying helpless on the floor beside a stool occupied by cowboy boots. She could be kind and let the man know, but instead, she takes three quick steps; her last one smothers the bill and drops her purse as if it were an accident. With one smooth fashionable squat, she grabs both her purse and the hundred dollar bill while Cowboy Boots groans in defeat to the dealer. Rising, she sees he's miserably losing at blackjack, down to his last few chips and his old face held heavy in his hand. She slides onto the stool next to him, effortlessly, placing down his hundred on the felt as if it were her own, and in many ways, she can justify how it is.

"When in Rome, make lemonade, right?" she says, thinking that's how the saying goes.

As her chips are pushed across the felt to her, Cowboy Boots ogles over her exotic features. She's aware of what her presence does to him. She's aware of what she does to most men and uses it to her advantage. She needs all the advantages she can muster. Her current situation demands it. She pushes her long wavy black hair back over her shoulder, revealing her black slinky dress that doesn't try to cover much nor hug much either. Then places a cautious bet before stopping a passing waitress.

"Champagne, please."

But what she doesn't see is the man from the craps table, with his gaze still transfixed upon her. She turns back around as the dealer checks for blackjack. Nope, the dealer shows twelve, draws a king, dealer busts.

"Hey, I should call you, lady luck!" Cowboy Boots yelps like he won a ribbon at a rodeo.

"If you only knew what they actually call me," she says as if it's a joke, even though it has never made her laugh before.

Over at the craps table, it's his turn on the dice. He stands alone and stands out among a table filled with t-shirts and shorts. From a distance, he's all style, with an aura of celebrity. A short-sleeve sweater fits perfectly over his broad shoulders and wide chest, and his jeans are cuffed neatly over his black engineer boots. But up close, there is more substance to gauge. Healed scars formed like fossils of time embedded into the gaps in his cheeks give him a menace. He'd be threateningly handsome if it weren't for the scars—something that has plagued him almost his entire life. He loads the dice in his palm and jiggles them for luck as if luck were a craps game too.

"Let's go, Scarface, make me money," screeches a shabby guy in a Lake Havasu t-shirt flanked by a bunch of the same.

He clenches the dice with a concealed fury. His eyes glare severely at Lake Havasu until he lets the dice fly off the back wall of the table.

"Crap out," the dealer cries.

He's not surprised to lose at the pass and runs his fingers through his thick dark pompadour like a remedy for calm. Scooping up his chips, he ignores the stares and gripes from the Havasu flock, and magnates toward the blackjack tables, more specifically, toward the dark-haired beauty.

"Blackjack," she cries softly and smiles like she's almost forgotten how to, but then suddenly, her smile fades at the sight of the dealer's ace. "You wouldn't dare," she threatens, and the dealer flips a five then doles out their winnings.

"Good win," asserts old Cowboy Boots.

"It's only a matter of time, though, isn't it?" she replies. The dealer silently agrees.

"I wish I could stay," Cowboy Boots says, pushing his chips forward before rising with a grimace for his rickety knees. But before the cowboy leaves, he tells his incoming substitute, "You're a lucky guy."

The man with the thick dark pompadour who ventured over from the craps table runs his hand through his hair again, waiting, giving the old-timer his space and time to depart. Then he's quick to put his chips down on the other side of her and see if the old coot is right, but the treasure he's seeking is turned away toward the incoming waitress. He places a generous bet and strokes his scars, knowing they're not so readily accepted by beautiful women. She turns back with her champagne and looks to her new table partner. *Damn,* he thinks, *she's intoxicating* and studies her more than a decade younger face to see if his scars turn her off, but her focus is direct and deep, and his heart races.

"Sir?" the dealer pleads for his attention.

He looks down at a pair of eights, trying to remember the math and what number you hit in blackjack when his dark-haired beauty fires in, "Split." He hears her suggestion, but he's immobile. "Trust me," she says, and to him, trust is a word better done than said, so he adds chips for the split.

"Been a while since I played this game," he confesses.

Looking down at his stacks, she notices the plethora of black and blue chips he has in addition to his red and white, and figures him for a craps man, a man who plays the field.

"What's your game then?" she asks.

"Don't have one," he remarks while eyeing her like she could be his game.

Their stares are like silent threats, daring the other to engage in this foreplay, and neither one admitting to their undeniable connection.

"Dealer busts," they hear the dealer say.

"So you do have game," she says, referring to his winning hand.

He slides her a ten-dollar chip from his winnings. He figures she's more than earned it.

"What a gentleman," she purrs. "Thank you."

He looks down at his new hand, a king queen, like he's been rewarded. "I guess being a gentleman still pays."

"We'll see," she says suspiciously, in case he's speaking about more than the game. She looks down at her two and four of hearts, not surprised. She's been dealt low cards for more than a few years now, so she knows how to dig in for a fight—that's what she does.

He watches, narrowing in on her with his eyes like long lenses, seeing her emotion telling details—that's what he does. He's captivated with her every expression, her perfect skin, the slightest of facial movements. Capturing the image of a film star from decades-long gone, and he wonders her story. She hits for her next card and the next. Her expressions, going from hope to despair and back to hope, as if despair never appeared, because she's almost there, her four low cards add up to eleven.

"If I were lucky, I'd get a face card," she says, testing fate, but in her head, she's betting against herself—at least then she'll be right—so she calls forth her destiny, and it's a four. Only there's no celebrating because it means she'll lose. How could she not? She has five small cards in front of her. There's no question the next card is a face card, the story of her life, doom lurking around every corner.

He's thrilled to watch her strategize, observing the mental pinball going on behind her intense eyes. He's never been much into games but watching her play this out is like witnessing a good pitcher on the mound. He's rooting for her.

She wants to motion stay and keep herself in the game but staying on sixteen isn't how she plays. She's compelled to play out the hand for the sake of the table, at least. If she doesn't hit, she'll affect the deck's entire rotation, changing the outcome of their next few hands, who knows what else, and she knows why staying idle is a bad idea. So she hits, and he watches with anticipation. Another four, so that makes twenty! She can't believe it. He's quick to motion stay to the dealer, and the dealer turns and flips so fast he can hardly keep up with the math. It's not until the dealer calls out, "Dealer bust," and pays out that he realizes she won. They won. He looks to her to celebrate, but from her only slightly curled smile, he sees she's more relieved than celebratory.

"You really worked for that one," he commends her.

"It should have gone the other way. The odds were against me," she says with torment, her head slightly down.

Suddenly he sees her broken pieces spill out from under her elegant facade. This beauty is hiding a painful past, dark corners, and hard nights, and strangely enough, it only makes her more attractive. He wonders what the hell she's been through and how she made it through while maintaining her grace and beauty.

With a reflective tone, he adds, "The odds are always against us."

"Isn't that the truth," she says, pleasantly surprised to be relating with him on a deeper level. With his clean and crisp style, she initially pegged him for a slumming Bellagio brat, but as he smiles back, she suddenly finds herself wondering who he is and what this is. They play the entire next hand linked in gaze, and she's unable to read him. Is it a deeper connection, is it a game of flirtation, or, she wonders, is it something more sinister?

The call, "Dealer busts," breaks their stare, and more chips are slid across the felt to them.

He can hardly believe his fortune. "That old man was right," he claims, putting half of his chips in, tripling down on the currency of her luck.

But she pulls her chips and tosses back the last of her champagne. "Well, that's all she wrote."

He thinks she can't be leaving. It doesn't add up, but for him, nothing's adding up lately. He calls out, "You're done? We haven't lost."

"I double, I walk. I don't push my luck."

"But we're winning."

"My luck runs out just like that. I get by only because I'm getting better at predicting it."

"Sir?" the dealer interjects.

He looks down at a jack two and looks to her. She stands firm with folded arms, assuring him she's not going anywhere, at least until he plays out his hand. Focusing back on his cards, twelve is so far from twenty-one, so he hits, but it's a bust. "Shit," he calls out, seeing her already walking, so he scoops his chips and catches up. "I'm Carney."

"Hi, Carney. I'm Pru."

"Pru like in Prude?"

"As in Prudencia Romiti. Watch what you're getting at, Pal," she teases. "I only have sex on second dates."

Surprised by that, he tips his head and says with a Bogart-like voice, "Well, how long you in town?"

"Leaving now. Too bad for you," she says. But her eyes tell a different story as she approaches the teller first, placing her chips on the counter.

"What were you in for?" he asks. "I mean, no one comes to Vegas unless they have to."

"Let's just say, a wedding," she meanders.

"Why just say?" he asks, unable to take his eyes off of her.

She looks at him suspiciously. "You a PI or something?"

"A private investigator? No," he says curtly.

She laughs. He's obviously not a PI.

"The bride gave me the wrong day, wrong month, actually," she says, collecting her money.

He turns in his chips to the teller. "That's fucked up."

"It could be unintentionally on purpose," she admits, "but since I have very few friends, I can't afford to think that way."

He takes her in like a good movie but knows if he doesn't act quickly, she'll be out the door, and he'll have nothing but the celluloid of her in his head.

"Well, I have an extra ticket for the Cryptid Animals tonight," he throws out as he collects his money.

"What's the Cryptid Animals?" she asks, walking again.

He joins her, step for step. "A heavy metal band."

"That still exists?"

"Come and see," he says luringly.

She watches him walk beside her, in step, and she's in control. She starts to wonder if he would be a fun mouse to play with. From his hefty stack of chips at the table, she knows he's not a total louse, but she can't be sure yet. A mouse can easily be a beast.

"You know," she muses, "you should have stayed on jack two. The dealer showed fifteen. Luck is only part of it."

"Something tells me you could teach me a few things," he says before following her into the diner like she knew he would. "Vegas must be your town, and blackjack your game, huh?" he insinuates as they migrate toward the back of the restaurant like familiar strangers and slide into a corner booth.

"You could say that. I used to live here."

"I bet there's a story in that," he encourages, and by the look on her face, he knows he's right.

The memory of those days is long behind her, although still fresh enough to repeat injury. Even if she does tell it, she reasons, he won't believe her. They never do. That's why she usually doesn't even bother, but there's something daring about this stranger. She thinks perhaps she will, for toying purposes, only just before she could, a waiter interjects with two menus.

"Hi, I'm Edgar. I'll be your server."

"Hi, Edgar," she says, beaming bright, a performance for his benefit. "Bring us your favorite item on the menu. We'll share."

"Alright, I know just the delight," Edgar exclaims eagerly.

Carney looks inquisitively at her as he hands Edgar back the menus. "And a beer. Any brand. I don't discriminate."

She follows with, "Champagne or water. That's all I drink."

The waiter nods before leaving, and Carney can't believe his luck. Feisty and exotic, a dangerous combination. He leans in, saying, "Do you always order for the man?"

"I do what I want," she exclaims, "and I want good service. Plus, there's too much wasted time looking at a menu when all you do is order the same thing, and what's the excitement in that?"

"I would bet there's nothing but excitement in your life," he surmises.

"I see your game," she calculates. "You bet on people. Right now, you're betting on me. Only I'm not paying out for you later tonight." She leans back into the booth, twisting her torso in a way that moves the slit of her dress up, tantalizing him with more skin from her thigh.

As difficult as it is for him, he holds his gaze and teases back, "Can't it be more than that?"

She's heard that lie before and asks, "How about a little honesty?" Crossing her legs to show more skin, she toys with him even more. "Let's lay all our cards on the table and see how they fall. You can start with small suits if it makes you more comfortable."

He's eager to play and doubles down. "Alright, you seem like someone who's one bad experience away from getting a gun and shooting up a bank. Maybe you need a friend. And I'm not a bad guy to spend the night with."

She's taken aback. That's not the way she thought this was going. He is different, and different is exciting. She wonders if he really does see her that way or if he's just trying to tear her down to a size more reasonable. She deducts, "You must be attracted to danger."

His body language doesn't necessarily disagree. "Perhaps I see a similar hopelessness in you," he pecks.

"I look hopeless?"

"You look drop-dead gorgeous."

"Well, now we're getting somewhere," she pecks back playfully.

But he continues, "The world around you is dark and decaying. Sooner or later, your beauty will go, and then where will you be?"

"Hung out to dry and on the lamb looking for you," she smirks, playful or serious, it's hard for him to tell which.

"Wouldn't that be my fate?" he says as if his thoughts have spoken out loud.

The way he said "fate" makes her think they have something in common, but she knows the divide. He's in a far better spot than her. Most people are, and the ones who aren't are easier for her to spot. She wonders if perhaps that's why he's attracted to her, that her hopelessness will make him feel better. She figures he's betting on it, only he'll be setting himself up for disappointment.

"Dabble in self-sabotage much?" she asks.

Her question rips through his mind with enough truth for him to admit to, but denial is fast friends with the blissfully ignorant, so the thought rattles around in his head never making contact. Then Edgar drops in to deliver their drinks, and for Carney, there could be no more perfect timing.

"Thanks," he says, and Edgar smiles. They're his favorite table in the diner.

They both sip from their beverages, eyes locked in a game that neither knows the rules nor how to win, but neither can pull themselves away.

Taking his silence for agreement, she continues with her deductions, "I'd bet you make a habit of creating your own bad luck and place the blame onto the world. Why else would you chase after me if I'm as bad as you say?"

"Do you ever step away from the card table?" he asks, with laughter surrounding his words.

"Only on second dates," she confesses, hiding a smile.

"Something tells me you don't have many of those."

She gives him a look that tells him he may be right. Playfulness aside, it pleases her that he sees that, so often it goes the other way—treated as an object for sex. A curse and a blessing, depending on what she wants.

She admits, "Lately, it seems like love is a game where everyone plays dirty."

"You don't look so innocent," he quips, playfully, before realizing from her heavy eyes that the game just got serious.

She can't deny the truth in what he says. She lost her innocence long ago. The girl she used to be is a distant memory, and it's all her doing. She received a fast education for a cheap price, one she continues to pay for.

She insists, "Why don't you speed up this merry-go-round and tell me what you want?"

"I want to take you to a concert tonight," he says.

All she hears is the lie because that can't be all he wants. She doesn't know why truth is such a rare commodity. She hungers to tell him she craves honesty. Suddenly, Edgar drops in with a simple barbecue chicken dish.

"Here we go, bird's the word," Edgar says, with wide eyes as if he just dropped off gold.

Pru and Carney stare at the plate, uninspired, while Edgar waits for a reply.

So Carney chirps out, "That was fast, for chicken."

"Rotisserie," Edgar chirps back.

"Interesting choice," Pru chirps final.

"Enjoy," Edgar leaves, sticking to his decision.

Carney looks at her and wonders, "Is it ever what you think it's going to be?"

"Most of the time, unfortunately," she admits.

That resonates between the soft spots in his face. So often he's unimpressed with the expected, and that's why he's so impressed by her. He needs more, and he's secretly aching inside, wondering if she'll spend the night with him or leave him forever.

"Is he watching us?" she asks, devising a plan.

His eyes pan across the room, spotting Edgar watching them through the server station window. "Yep."

"Okay, take a couple of bites and smile at him," she says. "Then we'll head over to the concert."

He smiles victoriously. He may not have won his money back at the tables, but he won the night. She's not going anywhere just yet.

CHAPTER TWO

Carney stands at the Cryptid Animals merchandise table with a line forming behind him, scanning the back wall of devilish Chupacabra masks. First, pointing effortlessly to the scariest of the bunch, then pausing with contemplation before deciding on the one for Pru, a half-face black lacquer mask with horns.

"Are you sure?" questions the guy behind the merchandise table, but Carney's already decided. So the two masks are passed over the table to him in exchange for money.

Pru exits the ladies' room, startled by a swarm of men and women wearing mostly the same scary Chupacabra mask. *It feels like Halloween, but that's four days from now,* she tells herself as she tries to accept this weird world Carney has brought her into. Walking over to the bar, Pru wonders if this is one of those theatrical bands that pull an audience member up on stage for a ceremonial kill. While joining Carney and her waiting champagne, she sees a line of guys at the bar drinking their beers oddly by lifting their masks as if they're concealing their faces.

Looking at Carney, she says, "I'm not quite sure what I'm in for tonight. From the look of it, everyone seems ready to sacrifice someone."

"Only metaphorically," he admits. "Chet Swell, he's the lead singer. He thinks we should all kill the sheep inside ourselves."

"And here I've been killing them for years," she says, giving him a laugh.

He adds, "Oh, and there will be some fake blood."

"Oh, goodie," she coos sarcastically before taking a sip of her champagne.

She's not opposed to new or different experiences, but something about Carney has her nerves on edge. She can't figure out if she's chasing him or he's chasing her. All she knows is how she feels, and there's nothing casual about this encounter. She only hopes she can figure it out before she becomes the mouse to his cat.

"You know, that chicken wasn't half bad," he admits out of the blue.

She laughs with full agreement, saying, "No, it wasn't. We had Edgar all wrong," and wonders if she has Carney all wrong too; that perhaps good guys do exist, and he's one of them. It would feel refreshing for her not to play an angle, but the cynic in her thinks otherwise.

Suddenly, he gets an alert and looks at his phone and voices it out-loud without thinking. "6.7 earthquake off the coast of Japan."

"Interesting update," she says. And from the expression on his face, the seriousness, the look of concern, she wonders, "Meteorologist?"

"No," he says matter-of-factly, putting his phone in his pocket as if that could erase what he said. Then remembering, he pulls out the two masks from behind him on his chair. "Here. I got you one." He gives her the half-face black lacquer mask, taking the horrifying one for himself.

She doesn't see anyone else in her mask, and for a moment, she feels special. She puts it on and simulates a cute and sexy growl for Carney's pleasure, and he eats it up, giggling like men do when they see a sexy woman act like a little girl.

He adorns his full-face Chupacabra mask like most in the room and says with all seriousness, "I feel more handsome already."

"Because of your scars?" she wonders.

"And I thought you didn't notice," he deadpans her from under his mask.

She locks eyes with him through the holes. "I see everything."

"I saw you first."

"Are you sure about that?" she replies playfully, embodying the cat instead of the mouse, and then lifts her mask. "So what do you do, Carney? Where do you come from?"

"Suddenly, the mystery isn't enough for you? I'm a Chupacabra. I drink the blood of goats."

"Not exactly what I meant."

"I know. Who cares, though, right? It's more than likely we live in different time zones so let's enjoy the night," he says, feeling confident that she's the kind of girl who can take that sort of honesty.

"Look who's finally laying out some high cards," she doubles back, wanting more.

He stares at her dauntless face from under the protection of his mask. *If it's honesty she wants, it's honesty she'll get.* He shoots for a ten of spades, daring her to play on. "I want you to tell me your story. You used to live in Vegas?"

She takes a sip of her champagne, tasting his want. "I met a guy," she says as if that's how all of her stories begin. "He loved me for my brain and fed me with the food that love survives on and convinced me to move to Vegas to start a club crawl empire. Only his ambition was hungrier than his heart. And he was in the habit of making promises he couldn't keep, not only to me but to the wrong kinds of people, if you know what I mean." She motions to her nose like it's crooked, and he clearly understands. "And his car drove into the back of a flatbed truck, decapitating him upon impact," she says plainly and quickly without any emotion like ripping off a bandage.

He lifts his mask in disbelief or excitement; it's hard for him to know which. He's never met an angel who speaks with the kind of darkness she does, the kind he's only ever witnessed in fiction, the fiction his father comes from.

"Then they came to me for his debt," she continues. "What could I do, work the pole?" He looks at her, imagining she could. "It's not the nudity I have a problem with. It's the lap dancing. I'd make more money cocktailing. So I looked in the wanted ads and answered one... for an actress, a phone sex actress." His poker face gives slightly but only momentarily. She continues, "I thought what the heck, another odd job for my list. I paid them back and then moved out of state."

He doesn't know what to believe or if to believe, but it doesn't matter. He's fascinated by a good story, especially one with a female lead character. Usually, he's treated with masculine tales of criminal exploits and the ones that got away. The girls provide complimentary nodding and tittering giggles, only trying to play the part. It's so rare he finds a woman who's so graceful and yet so expository of her sordid past.

"I didn't know phone sex still existed," he cracks.

"There's an even greater need for a human to human interaction these days," she says with sincerity.

He wonders if she thinks herself a social worker for pleasing men on the phone and leans into the idea for comic relief. "An odd job with purpose?"

"Maybe, but I was too honest for that line of work."

He laughs at the dichotomy. "You're top banana in the shock department."

"Why, banana? Couldn't I be a papaya?" she wonders.

He laughs again, realizing she hasn't seen *Breakfast At Tiffany's*. But it was before her time, he reasons. "Were you any good at it? Phone sex?"

She eggs him on, "I don't know. Maybe you'll have to call me sometime."

His smile tells her he's thinking about it. She may not have him on the hook yet, but he's eyeing her bait with hunger. Suddenly the crowd descends into the theatre, like a wild pack of animals storming toward the watering hole.

He shifts his mood, becoming intense, chugs his beer, sets it on the bar, and lowers his mask. "It's time."

Following suit, she drinks down her champagne, setting it on the bar before lowering her half-face Chupacabra with an eye on him; she senses the change in mood and follows him slowly, almost hesitantly toward the auditorium. He pulls out their VIP passes and hooks hers around her neck. *VIP?* She questions her circumstance, her anxiety takes over, and she freezes, putting up her mask. “Are you sure I’m not the sacrifice? No one else is wearing this mask.”

But all he does is reach out his hand to her, expecting trust as the crowd streams past. She could take his hand and find out, and maybe it’s just a concert, or perhaps she is the sacrifice, and she’ll get pulled up on stage for some embarrassing moment. Would it be that bad? She’s hung around real devils, and these are just people in masks.

For reasons unknown, she takes his hand anyway and lets him guide her into the auditorium. A tribal drum track plays over speakers as they breeze through the crowd, past security, down the aisle to the front where their passes open up their VIP standing room only section, an arms throw from the stage. Looking back at the crowd, they’re all in one or two, sometimes three, different kinds of Chupacabra masks, and none with the one she’s wearing. They’re all doing a movement in unison. Their arms up halfway and moving them from side to side, like they’re holding onto bars in a cage, wanting their freedom. She looks to Carney, and he’s doing the movement too.

Suddenly, real drums replace the stereo track, the curtain opens to thunderous cheering and reveals a three-member band minus a frontman. The lead guitar player mirrors the crowd’s movement wearing one of the familiar Chupacabra masks, and that’s when she notices, all of them are in masks. And the drummer, a tough petite woman, bangs away on her set in a half-face black lacquer one, the same she’s wearing. Now she understands. She’s not the sacrifice. She just has the least popular mask. *That figures,* she thinks and lowers the black lacquer over her eyes with support. Carney nods his approval. She feels almost certainly now that Carney is the mouse, and it's her that's the cat.

The music elevates. The guitars sink into a deep hard hypnotic rhythm, and the crowd's movement accelerates. Then Pru notices the audience looking and searching behind them, and suddenly screams and cheers erupt as the middle of the room parts like the Red Sea. The lead singer makes his way from the back of the auditorium, entering through the opening of people, starting in on the vocals and whipping his dreadlocks to the beat before leaping gloriously onto the stage. She's stunned, watching him join with the movement of his flock, with his authentic tribal costume and Chupacabra mask—that's an elaborate version of what Carney and most in the room are wearing. He engages with their side of the auditorium, causing the audience all around them to cheer. Showing her appreciation, she claps her hands, but Chet singles her out and points to her. She insists to herself, she will not be pulled up on stage, but he's not asking for that. He wants her to do the movement and cheers her on. All eyes are on her, even Carney's. So she joins in, doing the movement too, and Chet Swell moves on with the rest of the show.

She turns to Carney and yells through the music, "I thought you said he wants everyone to kill the sheep inside, not be the sheep."

Carney laughs.

CHAPTER THREE

Alone in a dimly lit hallway holding onto her mask, Pru stands in ecstasy, with blood splattered on her face and neck. For a moment, who she is and what she's done is but a distant memory. All she can feel is the rush of life flowing through her veins like a transfusing of hope, thinking maybe she did need a friend, and he's not a bad guy to spend the night with. Then she sees Carney appear in a stream of light from an open doorway, waving her over. She goes to him with ease as if they've been together for years. He offers his hand to her, and she accepts so naturally like it's something they do. He leads her into a brightly lit, vibrant hallway where the band's crew members enter and exit, and acknowledges the band's security guy. The six-foot-five giant is an earnest black man with eyes that appear to always be looking out for trouble. Pru looks at Carney with wonderment as they follow the security guy through a labyrinth of doors and hallways to an open freight elevator. Once inside the steel box, the security guy closes the doors. Carney and Pru's eyes lock again, his blueish grey marbles and her brown beauties. They're in a communion of ecstasy in a bubble to themselves, and she doesn't want this night to end.

The security guy pivots his head around to speak. "I was a big fan of your dad's."

With Carney's eyes still locked on Pru, he says, "Thanks, man, appreciate it."

Pru wonders who his dad is.

"You probably get that all the time," voices the security guy.

"Hell, I don't mind. He's my pops."

From the way Carney looks at Pru, she can tell he could have this conversation in his sleep, but his demeanor is still kind and respectful.

The security guy pivots back again to add, "*Walking Alone* is one of my top five movies of all time."

Carney smiles. *Walking Alone* has a special place in his heart.

Meanwhile, the wheels are turning in Pru's head. It's been a while since she's seen that movie, but everyone has. It's that big.

"I had a small part in it," Carney elaborates. "I was the kid he gave the ice cream cone to."

Her eyes go wide.

"No shit," the security guy says, "after he smoked all those dudes at the DQ? How old were you?"

"Nine," Carney divulges, remembering how he nailed it in one take.

"That's badass," the security guy remarks. "You mind if I get a shot of us?" He pulls out his phone.

"Not at all."

Carney lets go of her hand and leans over so the guy can take a selfie of them.

"Thanks, man," the security guy says as the elevator door rings open. "Follow me. It's Carney, right?" Carney agrees and follows after him with Pru by his side.

Pru leans into him and whispers, "You kept that ace up your sleeve."

Carney flashes her a shy grin and strokes his pompadour. He knows his father's name is the ace women love to hear.

Pru grabs Carney's hand with a little more affection this time. Their journey inside this hotel labyrinth continues down another hallway, through another door to a suite with more security, and this is where their security friend leaves them. "Enjoy your night." He departs with those words as they drift into a prodigious suite where VIP cryptids mingle.

"Carney McMorris!" is yelled across the room, and instantly Pru realizes who Carney's father is. Mitch McMorris. An enormously famous actor, Oscar winner, and notorious ladies man later in his life. She knows she's flying at a different altitude by being with Carney and worries it'll show.

Approaching with an angelic presence is Chet Swell, the lead singer, in a Hawaiian surfboard shirt, eating from a bowl of strawberries. "It's a good thing I left you two tickets," he says to Carney, giving him a shoulder hug before turning his attention to Pru. "Hi there, I'm Chet."

She shakes his hand. "Pru. Nice to meet you. The show was amazing."

"I've left Carney two tickets for the last ten years, and you're the first guest he's brought. He's a lone wolf stubborn to adhere to his basic needs."

She wonders why that is. Is Carney a notorious ladies' man like his father?

"My needs are met just fine," Carney refutes.

Suddenly pensive, Chet leans in and unloads, "All of our needs will soon be in question in the near future. Society has a big decision to make. It could go either way. Survival of the fittest," he points to his head, "in these times of change. Grab another cryptid and head for the hills."

Carney looks concerned. "Do you know something we don't?"

"Just vibing what the world is telling me."

She throws in, "What's cryptid mean?"

Carney answers for his friend, "Mythical beings whose existence is questioned."

"Carney was born a cryptid," Chet adds. "What about her?"

"I only date other cryptids," Carney declares.

"I see," she says, realizing she might have hooked her fish after all. But it's not a clear path to reeling him in, so she teases, "This is a date?" Carney looks playfully back at her.

That's when Chet realizes, "Ah, you two just met."

Carney admits, "Ya. She picked me up at a blackjack table."

"If that's the story you want to tell," she quips.

Chet stares at the two of them. "I gather it's somewhere in between." Then he leans in between them and says, "I suggest you get to know each other fast. Love's the ticket for the next ride." His words like a secret gift, a gift unknown, and both Carney and Pru are momentarily paralyzed by it.

"Hey, Chet?!" a band member beckons from across the room, so Chet directs himself toward the call.

"Chet, before you go," Carney barks.

"Yeah, man?"

Carney gets in step with him and leans in to speak privately. "What did the band think of my concept for the video?"

Chet puts his hands to his heart to show his friendship before giving the bad news. "It's rigid and constricting and caged in. Not what I was expecting. I'm giving it to you straight, man, because I love you." Carney forces a smile, accepting the honest rejection with humility, and watches his pal, the rock star, mix in with his musical flock.

Then turning his attention back toward Pru, only she's not there!

Looking through the crowd, only to see every dark-haired girl could never be her. Checking the bedrooms brings him no luck. She's not in the hallway either. He goes back into the suite to check the bathroom, but it's occupied, so he waits anxiously. When the door lock sounds and the door opens, he's only more distraught that it's not her. Desperately leaving the suite, he traverses the labyrinth to the best of his memory, finding the security guy that brought them up in the elevator.

"Hey man, did you see the girl I was with?"

"No, man. Sorry."

He takes the achingly long elevator ride down, all the while wondering what happened, wondering if she heard his occupational rejection and lost interest.

Entering the auditorium again, it's mostly empty but for the stage crew stripping down the stage. Carney looks for her by the bar where they had their drinks. Only a bartender filling stock. He peeks into the ladies' bathroom, to the shock of some girls.

"Pru?"

"Hey!" they say back, so he leaves.

Back at the Ellis Island Casino, he looks around the now packed blackjack tables to no avail. He's lost in a crowd of strangers searching for her, and she's nowhere to be found. Maybe she doesn't want to be, he wonders, so he gives in and makes his way to his hotel room.

Standing over the end of his bed, he imagines the miserable night he'll have here if he stays, thinking only of her sudden departure. So he slips on his black leather motorcycle jacket and gloves, picks up his leather overnight bag, grips his full-face motorcycle helmet, and exits his room. The door shuts loudly and echoes in his head as he walks defeatedly down the hallway of harsh light to his shiny black Victory Hardball motorcycle parked under a light in the lot.

"Oh, look who it is," a voice shouts at him. "Hey, Scarface, where's my money you lost me?!" chides the craps player, the one with the Lake Havasu t-shirt, from outside a hotel room door with two others of his ilk.

"Fuck off," Carney shouts back and continues walking, but Lake Havasu chases after him with a threatening posture. Carney turns and sends him to the asphalt with a hard right to the face. His drunk boy-crew throw their cheap beer to the concrete and rush over to defend their friend, and Carney pulls a black 9mm handgun.

"Don't even try it," Carney dares, and his eyes say he'll do it.

They quickly back off, so Carney conceals his gun, fits his helmet, mounts his motorcycle, and rides off.

The bright neon of the strip reflects off his helmet concealing his loneliness from the masses. Riding fast on the lonely road, he leaves Las Vegas behind but not from his mind. Getting her out of his head is an impossibility. He replays their entire night, and every word said, clues that layout like an unsolved-mystery, one that, if left unsolved, will torture him. He can't figure where it went wrong. Their banter was fun. Even the heavy stuff was responded to with playful delight or a kind reception. Why would she leave? Was it Chet's words of advice that love's the ticket? Or maybe she was lying the whole time. She's a call girl and had to go back to work. *Fuck!* He could play this game all night—that's what he does.

An accident ahead forces him to get off and take a detour, so he descends into Los Angeles to take surface streets the remainder of the way. He passes its forgotten landmarks and late-night debauchery outside nightclubs and all-night fast-food establishments. It occurs to him she could have been kidnapped from the party, maybe by someone she knew from her days of living there, and he wonders if he did the right thing by leaving. Should he have stayed? Does she need help? He lifts his visor at a stoplight and takes a calming breath reminding himself that he only just met her. He has no ties of responsibility to her. She's gone.

Continuing west, he rides toward the ocean. Only there's no ocean to be seen in the dead of night, only the blackness of the void beyond as he rides along Ocean Avenue to Rose Street in Venice Beach. A short turn before another onto Speedway, and with a click of a button, he rides his motorcycle into his garage parking next to his beautifully restored 1978 Chevy Nova, black with white-wall tires.

Entering his dark home, he flicks on a light. It's out. He opens his large stainless steel fridge. There's only beer, but he keeps looking anyway while the light from the refrigerator shines on his dad's *Walking Alone* movie poster on the wall. "Featuring Mitch McMorris" in a bold white font over his father in a long black trench coat with eyes that stare into your soul and a tagline that says how he feels: "We All Walk Alone." The light fades off his father's face as Carney closes the fridge and opens the freezer door, only Hungry-Man dinners, not what he's looking for tonight. What he's looking for can't be satisfied, but then he thinks, maybe it can.

Opening his laptop on the kitchen table, he searches Google for Prudencia Romidi. Trying all kinds of different spellings. Prudence Romiti, Prudencia Romitti. Nothing. Then he goes to his built-in humidor, pulls a cigar, and lights up when a notification alerts him. It reads, "Attempted Burglary in Venice Beach at Speedway and Rose." That gets him up to check the double lock on the back patio sliding door. Standing at the large table by the window, he looks out into the darkness. His face, greased in sweat. Puff, puff, puff, blow. He ruminates in a swirl of cigar smoke. The thoughts of something promising are long passed by, like wounds over healed scars.

Years before these fossilized gaps formed on his face, he remembers back to when he was that nine-year-old kid who once sparkled in his father's spotlight. Having never worked with his father before, he was looking forward to riding with him in the car that morning to the set, hand in hand like the prodigal son, but was surprised when his mom told him they would meet him there later in the day.

After costume and makeup, he and his mom were finally escorted to the makeshift Dairy Queen set, three walls dressed for the 1950s with actual candy on the counter. He was ready. After all, he's Mitch McMorris's son. Then he sees his dad, in that long black leather trench coat, like the hero that walks through the smoke machine, the dust clouds around him. His dad was always cool and relaxed with a pinch of intimidation, but he could sense his father's nervousness that day and knew it was for him. They practiced the scene at home, handing back and forth a wooden cylindrical case of pick-up-sticks as if it were an ice cream cone, but this was the real deal.

"The director shouldn't have to film your practice, so be ready when he calls 'action,'" his dad advised him before "action" was called.

Then his dad aimed his Colt revolver at the bad guys, firing off blanks until the actors leaped back onto the ground using their own propulsion. Smoke and dust drifted to the ground, and his father's eyes locked onto his; this was his moment. He looked at his dad like he could cry, and just before he does, his father handed him an ice cream cone as if it would make it all right, and it did. His face beamed for his closeup.

Although, now he knows an ice cream cone would never make it all right. He will always be a shadow in his father's world. Even his beach house is a reflection of him, almost untouched since when his father lived here. A tear slowly streams down his cheek, and he touches it as if it's coming from the past to comfort him. Staring out into the moonless night, he wonders what went wrong. He had promise as a young director but had some bad luck and bad timing when he got his big break at a decent-size budgeted film. He's always had a little bit of bad luck and bad timing, a shadow away from shinning.

CHAPTER FOUR

It's just after sunrise when Pru drives her beaten car through the quiet Hollywood Hills neighborhood. The drop-offs are steep, and the roads are narrow as she goes up the hill, but then after a turn, soon enough, she's on the decline again. This course is much like her life, a roller coaster of roads and turns. The only difference is that here she knows where she is going. As she parks in front of an old Hollywood Hills mansion, she begrudgingly takes in her surroundings. The weeds are overgrown, and the house paint is chipped, but she imagines it was grand in the '70s.

She walks up the steps wearing the same slinky black dress from the night before, carrying a bag under her arm, using her hip for support. Traversing the unclean path speckled with rocks and tree bark, she's not thrilled to always be coming back here, but her choices are becoming more scarce. Sometimes she wonders what will come first, her running out of choices or her desire to do something about it. She'd like to bet on the latter, she's feeling motivated lately, however she knows all too well that most anything can derail momentum.

Reaching the big Balinese door, she keeps ahold of her bag as she gives it a forceful thump. A half-naked blonde opens the door, squinting from the light, and blurts out, "Well, if it isn't the black widow," knowing Pru detests that nickname.

Forgoing the usually witty rebuttal, Pru attempts to get through, but the blonde blocks her way. The last thing Pru wants is a confrontation; she's exhausted and hasn't slept all night. From the way the blonde's face twists with conviction, she can tell this isn't over for a mile. Pru could demand the blonde ask what the owner of this house thinks of her blocking the door, although that seems pathetic and weak. That's not Pru's style, so she tries to enter again when the blonde pushes on her bag. The bag loosens from Pru's grip and falls to the ground.

"What makes you think you can come and go like you pay rent?" chides the blonde. "You're not special."

Pru doesn't think of herself as "special," but she knows she's better than this. She fantasizes about hitting the blonde in the face but knows it would most certainly mean her expulsion. Too tired to figure out where else to sleep and too tired to let this blonde get one over on her, she picks up her bag and walks past the blonde with an offensive force. Giving way, the blonde weakens her position, enough room for Pru to enter.

The blonde hurries back to the bed belonging to the man of the house who will give her nothing she wants. He is not kind. Although he may be generous, it's only because he expects something in return. Pru can see that's what he is all about. She has the capability to see inside of people, maybe not always instantaneously, but eventually, and her assumptions have proved correct. She only wishes the innate awareness stopped there, that it wouldn't apply to herself. She despises seeing the dark tar and cobwebs of her core, this twisted moral mush that morphs into whatever it needs to be to survive. It's not how she wants to live her life.

Throwing her bag down on the small guest bed, she lies on her back and thinks of Carney. She googles him to see his picture and doesn't read a single word written about him or his father because she doesn't believe a person can know another by what someone else wrote. Then she pulls out a notebook from her bag, finds a blank page, and puts pen to page.

> unseen by choice,
> Or for protection,
> She flies.

CHAPTER FIVE

Carney sits at his favorite haunt with his laptop open in a grey plume of his own smoke. It could appear that he's hard at work from the outside, but he knows the sad truth is that he's anything but productive. He turned in his last project a few years ago. It was a motorcycle club script that dove into the origins of the culture, the tightly knit group of renegades formed in the '40s after World War II. His father rode with the Hells Angels on occasion, and they visited on set, so he had a lot of resources and access to some of the clubs up north. He hoped the project would catapult him to a higher level, but his script got tied up in a studio merger. His bad luck and bad timing once again put his future on hold. Since then, he's been submitting for directing gigs, mostly tv, and the only thing bouncing his way are kind rejection emails. His saving grace is a weekly teaching position at Santa Monica College on Tuesday nights. Although it only emphasizes the point that those who can, do, and those who can't, teach.

When he was productive, his routine was a quick breakfast and off to this place, Hemingway's Cigar & Bar. A California Key West style cigar lounge with white wood walls and deep shadows from barred windows. He's been planting his flag here for so long he can't remember when he first visited, and when writing, he'd settle in the back corner in a large sofa chair and type away on his laptop for hours at a time. Always smoking a cigar while doing so, but lately, at Hemingway's, he's been just hanging out with a group of guys who like to hang out. Most are in the industry, or on the fringe of it, and have lots of time to dream and smoke.

Today he's chosen a chair by the windows where he's never sat before, distancing himself from everyone and anyone, and puffs away while glued to his phone. He searches social media for #PrudenciaRomiti, nothing; #PrudenceRomiti, nothing; #PrudenciaRomidi, and still nothing. Loneliness lingers on his face until he's abruptly interrupted.

"She's hot, huh?"

Carney looks up, saying, "What?"

His handsome friend and actor, Danny O'Brien, stares down at him with an unlit cigar between his teeth, adding, "The model I took to the party last night."

"I'm not looking at your insta story, Danny," Carney retorts.

Danny, a solid six-feet and could swim in the same gene pool as James Caan, settles in the seat next to Carney, and from the corners of his mouth, he says, "Speaking of stories, when are you gonna write again?"

Carney doesn't have an answer. It's not that the thought of writing something hadn't occurred to him. That's who he is, it's how he was raised, it's in his blood, but the world told him, film after film, that his voice doesn't speak to the masses. Telling Danny this would only put his friend in the position of exaggerated reassurances, and he doesn't need a false ego boost. So he stays silent while connected to his phone.

"Mark threw me his latest draft on the script," Danny says, knowing it would get a reaction from his longtime pal.

Inside, Carney is raging. He remembers when experience and due diligence were the stepping stones toward a respected career, and it angers him that nothing's earned anymore. The steps are shorter and slicker, and the respect doesn't matter.

Carney lets out, "He calls himself a writer now, too?"

"Yeah. Apple Bottom read it and says it's pretty good," Danny redirects, but that doesn't tell Carney much. Apple Bottom is just another casual fling Danny passes some time with, and whose opinion is as valued as an old shirt. "Who knows?" Danny continues. Placing the script on the armrest like a cushion for his elbow, he takes a torch to his cigar.

Carney sees what he's doing. "Hey man, don't soft shoe me. You want me to read the thing, right?"

"You know I trust your opinion. My agent is shit."

"No one reads anything anymore."

"You do," Danny says, knowing he got him there.

Carney bounces back, "Hey man, I haven't directed anything in years. I teach community college. If I were busy, I'd tell you to fuck off."

"No, you wouldn't."

Carney smiles, unable to deny the truth.

Suddenly, Rocco, their frenetic Italian friend with a boxer physique, flies into their conversation in a plume of smoke and sits on the arm of Carney's sofa chair.

"Hey, did you read Millennial's comments on Mark's thread? Keyboard Tough Guy's at it again."

"That kid better watch it, man," Danny says, referring to Millennial and adding flame to the fire, "he doesn't want to poke the bear."

Carney could care less about this conversation of social media drama, but he's stuck in the middle.

Rocco bangs on, "Marks's no bear. He's a rat!"

"How's that?" Danny rejects.

"I heard he was transporting some weed on a film he produced in Mexico," Rocco dishes. "He was the only one who didn't get arrested. You tell me what that says."

"You heard?"

Rocco doesn't reply back to Danny, choosing to speak to Carney instead. "How'd it go in Vegas? You get the gig?"

"Lost the music video and lost at the tables. Nothing new, man."

Rocco's empathetic-warrior nature heard too much. "Jesus, bro, well, cheer up. Fuck. We're all struggling. Don't drag us down."

"Hey!" Danny says, protecting his friend.

"Hey, what? He's my friend, too," Rocco says and then rallies the group with motivational clapping, "Look up, 'kay, let's go, bro."

Elite partygoers stream in and out of this mega-million dollar modern Bel Air home. Art and performance pieces are staged throughout. All the walkways and rooms are illuminated by bright lights steering guests through like an exhibit. Pru is fully nude, frozen inside a giant hand sculpture, and painted plaster eyeballs are stuck to her body, covering her most vulnerable places. Seeing the celebrities and industry who's-who's, she scans the room for Carney, knowing it could be a possibility.

No vision of him yet, so she keeps looking, moving only her eyes. There's only so much she can see from where she's been placed, and she has hardly any gawkers. She figures her art piece isn't very poignant, but there's also the consideration that she's between the entrance and the bar. The only people she sees with drinks already in hand are coming to use the nearby bathroom, where a slick man in his late thirties walks out with a beer, wearing an expensive loud-pattern sports jacket. She figures it's Versace, only his zipper is wide open, exposing his quite colorful boxers. She thinks about not telling him, although her boredom takes control.

"*Tssss,*" she says to him while holding her position.

Slick isn't sure he heard something, his eyes jet for a visual.

"You," she whispers loudly.

He finally locates her. "Me?" he asks with a boyish smirk.

"Your fly," she says and throws in a wink, so he's not embarrassed.

He zips up, looking at her almost pervertedly. "Do I know you?"

"No one knows me. I'm cryptid."

"You're one of Doug's new girls?"

"I'm no one's girl," she asserts.

"Even better, maybe I'll make you my girl," he suggests like she's something on a shelf he can buy.

She wants to tell him to fuck off but lingers a moment knowing she has no right to feel offended. After all, she's the one who's paid to be a naked art piece, and he's the rich white guy who paid to get in.

"Maybe I'm a woman between the devil and a dark alley and could use more understanding than judgment."

"I get it," he says, "you're getting out of the business. Catch you on the fly, Eyeballs."

He winks back and cocks his head like a riled rooster and walks off, leaving her with hate-filled eyes.

It's just past sunset when Carney enters his home in the dark and flicks the light, but it's out. Sighs, it's all just lately a routine. Feeling like he's stuck in a hamster cage and running on the same endless wheel going nowhere, he opens the fridge for answers. Only beer. Then the freezer, and his trusty friends, the Hungry-Man dinners, smile back at him. He places one in the microwave, and while he waits for his food, he checks his emails on his laptop. His eyes go to the keywords and phrases: "Bad news," "this shit happens," "they chose another director," and "it's not personal."

"Not personal," he voices out-loud. "Then why say it?"

Stripping off his shirt, he tosses it toward the garage where his washing machine lives. Going shirtless is something he only does in private because his cystic acne scars continue down his chest and back. *Ding!* goes the microwave. Putting the plastic tray on a plate, he carries it over to the table and eats his tv dinner without any tv, thinking about Pru. Imagining that she left him in Vegas because she was there to rob a bank, he speculates she had to meet up with her team, wondering if it's sexist to think that she would need a team to rob a bank. It's only for reasons that banks are far more sophisticated to break into today. That's when it hits him. She could easily rob an old bank, as Bonnie did with Clyde. Then begins to put together a mental storyboard of an old-time bank somewhere in San Francisco in the '40s during World War II. He imagines her in costume with Lauren Bacall-like waves standing across the street from her intended target wearing a black pencil suit and dark shades. She takes a puff of her lit cigarette, then stomps it out with her black ankle boot and struts across the street toward the bank. As if he's on set with her, he directs her character inside his head. Watching her coming toward him as if she's coming to him, but then passes right by and heads for the bank.

He rinses out his empty tv diner tray and tosses it into the recyclables, goes to the fridge, and grabs a cold beer. *Pop, fizzle* goes the foam. It's music to his ears. Standing in the kitchen, he dares himself to write, not even knowing where the story is going or if it would be any good. Then suddenly, he wonders if he's trying to convince himself against this because all he hears in his head is the negative criticism, comparing his filmmaking prowess to that of his father's.

Over to his humidor, he selects a cigar from a brand of many, plucks out an expensive cutter from a cigar box of plenty, and expertly cuts his cigar into one of the ashtrays placed throughout, wondering if he'll ever see Pru again. The thought of her now seems like something out of a dream or a movie, a movie he might just have to write. Lifting the wooden bar stopper for the sliding glass door and unlatching the lock, he slides the door open and steps out onto his beachfront patio, a stucco enclosure surrounded by well-groomed hedges that don't constrict his view. Plopping down on the single-person sofa chair, he lights up the cigar from a torch lighter he pulls from his front jeans pocket. If he ever does see her again, he won't let her out of his sight until he gets her complete story. He needs to know how and why a woman like her exists.

He gazes out at the colorful haze of the horizon post-sunset. The beach is serene, beautiful except for some graffiti on a concrete barrier that reads "Venis Bitch." But Carney is transfixed on the distant horizon, as he does. The dream or goal isolates his vision and blinds him from reality, including the reasons why a long row of homeless tents are multiplying outside his patio. Lost in his head, he pulls out his phone and opens the Final Draft app, staring at it, contemplating the dive in until he selects New Screenplay, then begins to type.

FADE IN:

INT. 1940'S BANK (SOMEWHERE IN SAN FRANCISCO) - DAY

A dangerous beauty in a black suit strolls into a bank with a .38 Special hidden in a large handbag. Her name is Prudencia.

Thinking for a moment, it's been a while since he's done this—writing. Something's changed in him, and he doesn't know what it is exactly, but this isn't how he used to write. He used to outline everything and structure each scene as if he were building a home. The writing process wouldn't begin unless he had index cards lined up all over his place, broken down into story and character segments. Wondering if maybe that was his problem, structuring himself into a box he couldn't get out of, he decides he'll write freely this time and begins to type again.

```
She looks around, making sure she doesn't know any of the women
behind the counter. Their men are off fighting in World War II
while they are put to work, and Prudencia sees the opportunity.
Approaching the teller, she pulls the gun.

                         PRUDENCIA
            Hand over the cash, and no one gets
            hurt.

The teller freezes horrified.

                      PRUDENCIA (CONT'D)
            Trust me, sweetie, I've killed before.

From the coldness in her eyes, you can tell she has.
```

Pru sits on a beaten couch in the decrepit mansion, looking closely at Carney's Instagram posts on her phone. Her account, @Rui_Prui, is so mysterious it doesn't even have a profile photo, only a generic clip art of a person. Scrolling over cigar shots, bro's posing, and old family photos, she zeros in on a picture of a sunset with the caption, "Don't let the sun set on your dreams." Her fingers zoom in on the beach and the concrete barrier with the "Venis Bitch" graffiti. She takes a photo of her screen as a loud sniffing comes from across the room.

The half-naked blonde, she pushed aside the night before, is doing lines of cocaine off a mirror on the floor. Next to her is another girl painting her toenails. Lately, Pru's been wondering if this will become her life; instead of the cavalier, *I'm just visiting* mindset that she's been telling herself to feed hope into her heart that this existence will one day be behind her.

The front door opens, and in walks Doug, the master of this dilapidated home in the hills. He looks like a mix between a surfer, a rocker, and a corporate loser and holds boxes of small cameras.

"New footy cams for the fetish freaks," he sneers. "You can thank me later."

The nail painter rolls her eyes.

"Are we still getting hair and makeup for the party tonight?" asks the blonde.

"Better than that. Your whole body is getting painted," Doug replies, which is food for the blonde's ears as she gets up to go sunbathing in the backyard.

Doug unloads the cameras on the kitchen table and grabs a box of ziplock bags. Coming to Pru first, he opens the bag and holds it open for her. "You working for the party tonight?"

She puts her phone down and reaches up in her skirt. "No, I've got somewhere to be in the morning," she says, pulling down a pair of cotton and lace panties and puts them in the open bag.

"You found your next mark?" he speculates.

Pru glares back with disdain, thinking this doesn't deserve a response, and he moves onto the nail painter with another open bag while looking back at Pru in case she decides to play on. But Pru stays silent and goes back to her phone to eye some more of Carney's photos.

The next day, a dense marine layer still looms over the boardwalk in mid-afternoon. As Carney exits his beach house with his leather backpack draped over his shoulder, he makes sure the door's locked, checking it twice, before heading out onto the boardwalk and walking in the direction of Hemingway's Cigar & Bar.

Pru, incognito in jeans and a leather jacket, conceals herself behind a palm tree, near the homeless tents, watching him. *That was too easy,* she thinks. She only had to wait half a day.

Hearing a lighter flicker, she looks toward the tent. A homeless woman in french braids is cooking some heroin inside. The homeless woman's eye-contact tells Pru, *you're not a threat to me,* and for Pru, the threat is that the homeless woman's right. Pru has more in common with this woman than with Carney at the moment. But she's planning that's about to change.

Donning dark shades, she creeps out onto the boardwalk and follows Carney from a safe distance. He walks fast, so every once and a while, she has to jog a few seconds to catch up. She could simply wait by his house for him to return, but that would be too obvious. As he turns the corner, she cuts a diagonal and hides behind a palm tree in case he comes back around. When he doesn't, she strolls casually to the corner just as he enters a building. Looking at the sign, "Hemingway's Cigar & Bar," she realizes this is the place he's always posting from on his Instagram and figures now's the time to enact her plan.

Meanwhile, Carney enters into a smoke cloud and takes a direct course to Danny, who's sitting up at the bar, pulling out the screenplay Danny gave him from his backpack.

"I'm gonna shoot you straight," Carney says, handing over the script, "but let me just add I do not want to get in the middle of this."

"Shoot."

"Everything's one-sided. If this were a painting, it's painted all black."

"So, it's dark?" Danny estimates.

"No, dark is a feeling, a mood. It could be any color. It's one-note, is what I'm saying," Carney explains, while Danny contemplates his words puffing on his cigar. "Look, man," he continues, "I don't know what he has on you, but you got a career to worry about. And Mark's a greedy gull."

"What would your dad do?"

"My dad wouldn't do it. And if he was strong-armed, he'd strong-arm them right back."

"The heroes of your dad's time are gone, pal, sorry to say."

"Maybe it's time a few of them came back."

Danny ruminates with his cigar. "Maybe."

"Trust me," Carney says, not realizing he's saying Pru's words that to him are better done than said, and before he's pulled into any further discourse, he heads for the door.

"But you just got here," Danny barks out, recognizing there's something different about his friend but can't put words to it just yet.

Carney's out of the door without a response. He's got a new main character inside his head calling for his attention. And hoping a new surrounding will inspire some productivity, he dodges a couple of skateboarders out on the busy boardwalk before finding a seat on a bench by a small grassy knoll. Opening up Final Draft on his phone again, he begins to type.

EXT. PLAZA - DAY

She runs into a crowded area and

Then he deletes it and stares out at the busy boardwalk before he starts again.

EXT. TRAIN STATION - DAY

After receiving her ticket for L.A., she disappears into the sea of people, herding toward the trains. She heads for the Central Line, but her suit jacket is caught on a man's briefcase. Every pull shreds threads. The man is pleased to hook such a beautiful woman, but she wants free of his hook, now.

He strokes his scarred chin, thinking as he watches b-boys dance for tips, and throwback hippie artists sell tie-dye-inspired watercolor prints.

"Unseen by choice, or for protection, she flies," he hears a poet say from over a small speaker. "Fleeing from danger she sings, her blackened wings burnt from flight, but flies again despite the fright. Her cryptid eyes..."

Hearing the word cryptid, it's like a beacon calling out to him. He makes his way through the crowd surrounding the poet, and that's when he sees her. His breath escapes him, and his heart pounds. It's really Pru. He can't believe his eyes. Even in her casual attire, he thinks she holds the audience with an elegance meant for another time.

Looking down at her phone, she's yet to see him, reciting, "Haunting or calling, where did she go? Was she ever?" Her voice, amplified by a portable speaker connected to her phone, overly accentuates the vowels like a beat poet. "What truth she sees, so she flees. Unseen. Insane. Like a raven in the rain."

Then her eyes lift to the audience, and she sees Carney standing in the crowd. Her plan worked. Their eyes lock with intensity as she says the last line of her verse, "Unseen. In pain. Like a raven in the rain."

CHAPTER SIX

Pru peruses around Carney's home, slow and observant as if she were in a museum. "Not what I thought, for someone who stays at the Ellis Island Casino," she says, pleasantly surprised by how cozy his home is.

Carney discreetly empties some ashtrays. "A guy has his preferences," he replies, noticing her close observation of the *Walking Alone* poster as if it were a Rembrandt.

"Same eyes, you and your father," she says without looking back at him, and he wonders if she somehow memorized his eyes from their night together. She continues on, past the humidor and into the living room. "Interesting smell in here, like a secret social club, cryptids only."

He laughs at that because it's Pru saying it. If she were anything resembling the girls he's used to, he would take that comment as passive-aggressive, a gentle way of telling him she doesn't like the aroma, and maybe she doesn't. Then again, a woman like her would just say it. Will he ever know? He enjoys thinking that about her, and the enigma of her only excites his interest. She's like a foreign land, and he's the explorer, navigating her delicately, without intrusion upon her shore, for he doesn't want to be met with an attack. Only she's not foreign. She's a local. Although it never occurred to him before that she could live in L.A., it makes perfect sense now that he thinks about it. There's no way a girl such as her could exist in the middle of the country, New York or San Francisco possibly, but here she is in his living room.

"If I knew you lived in Los Angeles, I wouldn't have been so mysterious," he admits wholeheartedly.

"If you weren't so mysterious, I wouldn't have felt the need to be so poetic," she says, browsing his bookshelf.

He watches her eye a family picture of him when he was young on a western movie set with his parents. A time when they were happy, before his parents' divorce, and before the realities of life came flooding in too soon.

"Like a raven in the rain?" he repeats from her poem, and their eyes lock from across the room.

"I like ravens," she purrs. "They're intelligent and incredibly misunderstood." Her face lights up, and he can tell it's more than an infatuation with birds that gets her going. It's that she must see herself in these creatures and that she, herself, is incredibly-intelligent and misunderstood. He has no doubt. "They spend their youth in rebel packs until they find a mate," she continues, "and stay together till death-do-they-part." She looks at his face for a reaction and finds none, so she doubles down. "Shouldn't we all be so lucky?" her eyes ask with intention.

"Not for this rebel bird," he throws back, quick to calm her agenda. Surprised to see an oddly traditional side of her, he wonders if under all the eyeliner and stiletto soul lies a woman who longs for love. "I was hoping I'd see you again," he admits, appealing to her sensibilities. "I couldn't find you on social media."

"I choose not to be a target," she says with some underlying hostility. Then she briefly scans his father's Lifetime Achievement Award from AFI like museum-goers do when they want to get onto the next exhibit.

He estimates she was subject to bullying, and maybe that's where she gets her edge, or at least where it began to get sharpened.

"Some people have no choice when it comes to social media," he thinks of himself.

"We all have choices," she fires back.

He would like to praise her strength-of-character, but he can't abide by the notion that she only makes thoughtful and correct choices. Her decision to leave him in Vegas can't be high on her list, not to mention making an early exit from the blackjack table while they were on a winning streak. He decides to put her on the spot and bring light to the elephant in the room.

"So why did you take off in Vegas?"

She knew that question would be coming up, although she can't answer him honestly, not right now. She pulls a book on camera lenses from his shelf, perusing it casually like she's at a library. Something about delaying him from satisfaction pleases her.

"Maybe I'll tell you," she says coyly. "One day. We'll see."

He stares back with both fondness and suspicion, and, from the way he saw her swipe that hundred dollar bill from Cowboy Boots, he wonders if she's going to swipe his book in front of his eyes.

"Is it just coincidence that you're in Venice?"

She puts the book back. "You want the truth or the better story? Remember, though," she says sensually, "I'm nine nighty-nine a minute."

"So reading your poetry was an act? And I'm just a sucker?"

"No, I read poetry."

"For money?"

"Sometimes just for applause."

He doubts there's anything she'd do just for applause. Although he remembers her talking about phone sex like another odd job and speculates she's been trying a little bit of everything. Maybe poetry is just that. "Another odd job?"

"Sure," she says, looking at a red box marked EQ next to a fire extinguisher. "Is this an earthquake box?"

He nods assuredly, admitting it is as if it's no big deal, hoping she doesn't probe further into his tormented psyche.

"What's with you and earthquakes?"

Damn, she went there, he thinks before figuring how to downplay it. "Some things keep me up at night," he admits, anticipating that will be the end of it.

She senses his resistance and wonders if it is a fully loaded box, equipped for long term disasters. *How far does his paranoia go?* "You have cash in that box too?"

He wonders if she always has money on her mind. "Maybe," he lies, enjoying teasing her.

Back at the bookshelf, she looks at Chet's signature on a Cryptid Animals album and comprehends the complexities of Carney's personality. He's a wild, mythical man who's far more grownup and responsible than her.

"A man with one foot on the grid and another off of it," she assesses with a smile. He silently agrees, never before realizing that side of his personality, and watches her scan his bookshelf, looking for something before she finally asks, "Where's your father's Oscar?"

He used to have it on the shelf next to the AFI award but moved it as it represented the constant reminder of who he's not. He strokes his hair back, curbing a response.

"It's somewhere safe."

She takes that as it's not safe here, and she's relieved that he knows it. From how easy it was for her to find him, he could undoubtedly be a target for thieves who know what they are after. Interestingly enough, she's not even that intent on seeing it, but she's never seen one before. Then browsing the bookshelf again, she sees another award in the far corner. Upon inspection, she sees that it is his. She takes her time, honoring him, as she reads, "Palm Springs Film Festival" and "Carney McMorris for Directorial Achievement."

She's never been good enough at any one thing to be considered for an award. She's a jack of all trades, all low-level service industry trades. It's not that she couldn't have put her mind to something and achieved it, she was one of the top students in her class, but she has never been interested in just one particular thing other than men and poetry. Besides, the pursuit of life is taxing enough.

"What do you do for work now?" he asks.

This is not something she can answer so readily because he's living above ground with a bank account in normalcy, and she's rummaging beneath it with late nights and lunacy. Even his words want to put her into a box she doesn't fit into, so she skates around it, coyly. "This and that. Freelance."

He gives her a daring stare, holding back a smile as he says, "Now who's being mysterious?"

She smiles playfully, looking up at the stairs toward a loft, wondering what's up there. "Oh, I thought I was speaking your language," she says with laughter surrounding her words.

He admits, "Okay, I'll take that. After all, I dished it out," giving into a smile.

She circles the couch, passing the liquor cabinet to come closer to him. Feeling the electricity, she wants to be close enough so that the hairs on the back of her neck stand up and maybe even toy with him some more so he feels it too. But he evades her, circling the couch the other way so that they are slowly chasing each other. He likes this game.

"Want to go another round?" he challenges her.

"I'll play."

"Don't cash in early this time," he teases. "I think I've earned this second date."

She laughs. "You're feeling lucky."

A sudden burst of brightness hits the room, and he looks to the window. "The marine layer broke," he notes and peers out through the blinds to see the sunlight bouncing on the water. "Want to go for a ride on my bike?"

"Is that a metaphor?" she asks, with a one-track mind, not realizing he could be thinking about anything other than sex.

Metaphor it wasn't because she finds herself on the back of Carney's motorcycle, wearing a full-face helmet and face shield. Her arms are locked around Carney's midsection as they fly up the coastline toward Malibu. The blue ocean water glistens, and the sun glows nearer to the horizon. He pulls into a vista overlooking the ocean and parks, warning her not to burn her calf on the exhaust pipe and describes how to dismount, and she does.

The view of the sunset is magical. Mainly because it was a particularly cloudy day and the remaining clouds give the atmosphere texture. Still, she's viewing him instead. Feeling a bit exhilarated after the ride, she tries to calm the emotions she feels fluttering up inside her like a teenage girl. She reminds herself not to fall into his trap and teases, "For a guy who doesn't play games, you have a pretty standard practice. Take a lot of girls up here?"

He takes her helmet and secures it on his bars. "For a girl who likes ravens for being misunderstood, you got this bird all wrong."

She watches him take a seat on a rock and voices out loud the sad truth, "That would be a first," and joins him.

He looks out at the sun setting. The sun shoots ray beams through the clouds, and he's in awe of the majestic beauty that surrounds them like it's a sacred moment. And with a deep breath, she lets down her guard to enjoy it as well. Their bodies and minds embrace the silence with comfortable ease.

"Big things happen during sunsets," he explains. "The good guy gets away. The leading man grabs the leading lady for a kiss," he pauses, and for a moment, she thinks he's going to kiss her. But instead, he continues, "My father walked off to a few during his heyday. It's the golden hour for movie making." He stares in reverence at the fading light.

She realizes she's never met a man more enthralled by dramatics, and now she knows how to get him motivated. She stands up in front of him, blocking his view so that a shadow casts over his face, she wants all of his attention, and he looks up, wondering what she's doing. That's when she straddles him, swinging her legs all the way around him so her knees won't scrape on the rock. It's an incredibly intimate position, and as she runs her hand through his hair, she notices him blush. Her lips are intentionally close to his lips to give him the moment she's also been craving. The corners of his mouth turn upward, telling her he wants her too, but he doesn't make a move. "I don't know if you're my next bad luck or good bet," he says, "but I can't get enough of you."

She smiles victoriously for having him on the hook, but he's still not kissing her.

"I have to warn you," she states seriously, "I'm incredibly addictive, so don't take a sip unless you are prepared to commit yourself to the habit."

"Maybe I should start going to meetings now instead."

She dismounts from his lap in defeat and turns her back. But he grabs her arm like she's a leading lady and spins her into his lap for a passionate kiss as the sun boils into the ocean behind them.

Her kiss is even more deadly than he imagined it would be. Her lips are soft, and she tastes sweet like maple syrup. His thoughts are wild for her, and he imagines her story filled with broken hearts and lovers with empty pockets, but he's willing to pay the price for this ride.

Back on the motorcycle, her black helmet rests on his back again as they soar back down the coastline. She looks out at the horizon as the remainder of the sunlight glimmers faintly on the edge of the horizon. For the first time in a while, she's optimistic. Suddenly, there's a CRASH!! She hears metal and screeching tires, and as she turns to look, the motorcycle jerks forcing her to reset her grip. She doesn't see the point of impact but knows they were hit only because a shadow of a truck vanishes. All she sees now are chunks of saddlebag fiberglass dancing in the air in slow motion, and then her boot swings up in the wrong direction. Although, she feels nothing. When time catches up with itself, the motorcycle wobbles down the highway at high speed, so she grips even tighter out of concern she'll fall off. He glides the bike to the shoulder of the road. She knows her leg is broken but still can't feel any pain, so she slides off onto the high grass and stares up at the sky. Purposely, she knows not to look down, to have that image of her leg burned in her mind, and only to recall it again and again in torment.

He goes to her, falling to his knees with horror on his face. Her left leg is mangled as if she stepped on a landmine, and bones are protruding through her jeans. Struggling to unstrap her helmet, he loosens the strap and manages to get it, and slips it off her head while her eyes stare up at him.

"It's good to see everything's on even keel again," she chirps with a sweet smile.

"What?!" he asks, fearing she also hurt her head.

She explains, "We were pushing our luck."

He wonders if she's in shock.

There's commotion all around, people coming out of their cars and talking on their phone to the emergency. But the only sound she hears is the waves crashing on the beach below. There's calm all around her. She fully accepts that if she has to go, she wants to go with peace. Taking slow breaths, she is still not feeling any pain and looks up at the sky and sees ravens dance in flight until the wings of a helicopter whip into sight.

CHAPTER SEVEN

Carney sits silently inside the nearly deserted UCLA Trauma Center waiting area, his body quietly idling. At the same time, his mind races. He keeps looking at the clock, the ticking clock and its incessant *tick tick tick* that has his nerves on edge. 11PM, it reads, even though an hour ago it felt like it was 10:45, and if the nurse weren't chattering and clacking away like she's at a cocktail party, he would ask her again for an update. Then there's the *swish, swish, flop, flop* of the orderly mopping the floor next to the automated door causing it to open and close, again and again. His ears and eyes engage as if each sound is an unknown animal, and he's alone in the wilderness.

Now the clock reads 2AM, he's still in the same seat, and his foot has fallen asleep. He tries to shake it, but it doesn't move. Nothing's moving, except the hamster wheel that's running in his head. He questions Pru's calm acceptance at the crash site. Life was anything but even keel at that moment. While stroking his thick hair, Pru's enigma increases in size and feeds his need for knowing how she ticks. Little movements and sounds aren't triggering a reaction from him anymore. He's become desensitized by their lack of put out, so when the surgeon finally approaches, it takes him a minute to register he's there before he rises to greet him.

"Is Ruby your wife?" the surgeon asks.

"Ruby?" Carney quickly assumes it is her real name. "No. We just met the other day. Is she going to be all right?"

"We were able to save her leg. One more inch to the left, and it might have been a different story."

A different story that would have been, Carney thinks. The same film he's been playing on that hamster wheel all night. They were inches away from a tragic ending.

As he walks the hospital's solemn hallways toward her room, he thinks back to the accident, replaying the endless loop. He remembers the sound of a crash coming from up ahead on the other side of the road. Every sense in his body was alerted to the danger, running through his veins like molten lava. The harsh sound of death in the form of screeching metal just before the fishtailing truck came into his view, swooshing by him like the Grim Reaper's breath. He knew Death was present. He felt him knocking. Yet they survived his visit without a scratch to either of them, or so he thought.

The collision to the bike felt powerful, but he thought they were out of the woods, even though they were in a fifty-mile-per-hour wobble. Then he felt her grip his back, tight, holding on for dear life. He knew he had to bring her to safety to get her off the road. He remembers getting to the shoulder and her sliding off the bike's back and onto the grass. The kicking of the kickstand, he did it in one kick. He remembers he wanted to throw the bike to the side and run to her, but he couldn't. It weighs eight hundred pounds and could crush her. So he had to do everything right, just to get to her, and he did. It was hard to tell if she was breathing. His hands had to be gentle when he unbuckled her helmet strap, and he remembers slipping her helmet off as if her future depended on it. When he viewed her left leg for the first time, he thought it was gone, but then he realized it was snapped underneath itself. It was a vicious sight. Bones like broken tree branches protruded through her ripped jeans. When the paramedics arrived, they unfolded her leg from under itself like a rag-doll while she stayed calm, looking up at the sky. He wondered what she was looking up at, and when he looked up, there was nothing but blue sky.

Not knowing if this was his fault, he wonders if he could have done more. Stopping at the end of the hospital hallway, he sees Pru's room, number 1036. He enters so slowly his guilt arrives before his body into the darkened room, stopping a few feet from the foot of her bed. Paralyzed. All these anxious hours till now, he's finally having a view of her, and she's okay. Knocked out on drugs, she has a peaceful expression on her face, like a beautiful princess resting in a meadow, her skin pure and lovely without any makeup, but her left leg is wrapped heavily in bandages from hip to toe. Inching closer, like he's walking up to a viewing at a funeral, he walks beside her bed. Her breaths lift her chest, and his breath lifts with hers. Then he reads her hospital wrist band, "Ruby Romiti."

He doesn't know where she lives or where she even came from, it's like she fell out of the sky for him, and he wonders what the meaning is for all this. Sitting in the chair next to her hospital bed, he feels different, awakened. Watching her sleep, he remembers the long nights he spent thinking of her and now believes they will be bonded forever by this chance with fate, or the pushing of luck that she calls it. He doesn't know what her initial game was or why she's hiding behind a false name, but he's determined to gain her trust and get to know all her whys and wants. Wondering if maybe that's why they were hit but swiftly pushes that thought aside, realizing the weight of the day is finally doing him in. His thoughts aren't even making sense anymore. Sitting back in the chair, he lets the relief of finally knowing she's all right wash over him. His eyelids close, and his body weakens into slumber.

She awakens grateful to the dawn's first light, shining in through the east-facing window where two birds perch for a moment before flying off, one at a time. After looking down at her leg, thankful that it's still there, she sees Carney asleep in the chair and wonders if he's been there all night. A beeping goes off down the hall, alerting a frantic nurse to run past Pru's open hospital room door, and Carney awakens. His eyes widen on her with a smile, and there's a delicate stillness between the two of them.

"Hey," he chirps.

"Hey," she chirps back.

"Last I remember, I was flying over the ocean."

"They helicoptered you here."

She moves around uncomfortably in the bed, aware that she may not look as attractive as when he last saw her, but he rises, thinking she's in pain.

"What can I do? Do you need the nurse?"

"No. I need hair and makeup," Pru titters. Carney appreciates the humor, hoping her jovial attitude extinguishes any possibility that she blames him.

As she looks down at her hospital wristband that says her real name, he wonders if he should address it. Then she covers it with her hand, thinking she still might have a way out without having to explain it. Sensing her sensitivity, he holds off from saying anything. Instead, he strokes back his thick hair and asks half-jokingly, "What are the chances a spinning truck from the other way only hits your leg?"

"The odds," she says softly, and her words linger in the air around them.

"It could have been worse," he admits with deep sincerity. Thinking of all the many ways, and then wonders if Pru thinks that too because his own words are lingering longer than he'd like. "Is there someone I can call?"

She sighs. "I don't have anyone."

"What about your family?"

"My parents are gone."

"They passed?" he wonders if they have this in common.

But she looks pained. "It doesn't matter."

He thinks *there must be someone I should call.* "How bout a friend?"

She squirms, realizing she can't hide from his questions, so she begins to get upset. "You don't have to hover. It wasn't your fault, and I'm not your problem." She looks around the room for her belongings. "I'll be fine. I just need my phone."

He cringes. "Your phone didn't make it."

"That's funny," she quips.

"It's the truth," he says seriously. "You have anywhere to go? Where do you live?"

She attempts to hide the pure panic she's feeling inside, knowing there's no way he'll find her homelessness attractive. Then there's an even bigger issue than that. Where is she going to go? Arching her head back into the pillow, she searches for the answer, but to him, she looks like a dramatic actress feigning a response, and in true Norma Desmond fashion, she says, "Where does one live? How? Why?" He agrees. He's been thinking with similar philosophic tones all night. Then she stretches her arms out like a kid just woken up to remind him how innocent and helpless she is. Trying to explain, "I'm like a lot of young actresses out here living from couch to couch, only I'm not an actress."

He nods with absolute believability. "That's understandable. L.A.'s a harsh place for poets and dreamers."

She's relieved that it went over smoothly, while he realizes the problem still remains. He begins to pace, fearing the unknown and all the bad bets that could be made. It's hard to see the next move when the pots greater than the hand. Under his logic, he can't let her go without knowing she'll be taken care of, and if she doesn't have anywhere to go, then he can't let her go. Maybe it's his guilt taking over, but he feels indebted to her, destined to her.

Seeing his unrest, she reads it as his fear of disasters, like she could be an earthquake or a hurricane, although she has to admit the tropical force winds are within her. "I'm sure they'll send me somewhere to heal," she reasons with a pinch of reverse psychology. "They can't just kick me out with nowhere to go, right?"

"Is it Ruby or Pru?" he needs to know before he decides.

She fiddles with her wristband, knowing she can't tell him the whole story. There's not even a story. It's just something that's evolved throughout her life because of everything that's happened in her past. So she settles on playing it cute. "Ruby doesn't live in me anymore. She's like the sheep I've killed before." Batting her eyelashes at him, she emphasizes the familiar reference, letting him know their conversations are not lost with her. "So I called up my middle name," she continues playing cute, "that's what it's for, right?"

He wishes he could film her because she is genuine entertainment. Even in her injured state, he acknowledges, she finds the means to make him laugh, so he decides and tells himself it won't be that bad. Besides, he's karmically endowed. Not only does he have the means, but he's no stranger to being a caregiver. He was at his mother's side while she battled stage-four breast cancer until she passed a couple months before his eighteenth birthday. In comparison, this should be a walk in the park.

"You're going to stay with me," he demands. "I'll help you heal."

She feels devilishly pleased that it went her way.

CHAPTER EIGHT

Hops Gardner always shows up to help when the McMorris family is in crisis. Becoming the sturdy rock when Mitch McMorris faltered, Hops always picked up the pieces, and nothing was too big or too small. Their friendship spanned thirty-three movies and the passing of both of their spouses. On the big screen, Hops mostly played the role of Mitch's sidekick, which wasn't too far off from how they related in real life. Just before Mitch died a decade ago, he told Vanity Fair, "Hops Gardner's the best man a friend could have."

"This transient knows this is temporary, right?" Hops grunts out in a rough tone as his sixty-five-year-old frame braces for balance, lifting a boxspring with Carney in the unused upstairs loft of the beach house.

"She's far from a homeless girl in a tent," Carney clarifies and begins to back himself down the steps as Hops pushes forward from above.

"I'm sure that's what all of them said before they stole a tent and set up home base."

"Hops, come on," Carney fires back with some heat, defending his decision.

"She has nowhere to go, and she knows who you are. You come on," Hops attempts to enlighten his godson. "We don't want another situation like what happened with your father. I don't know if I have another one of those in me."

Carney knows all too well what Hops is talking about, even though he wishes he didn't. His father's philandering ways only led him and the whole family into a lot of unnecessary drama, for which Carney learned there's nothing more dangerous than a mistreated woman.

As they set the boxspring in the middle of the room, nestled on two sides by couches, Carney insists, "This ain't that."

Then they traverse back up the steps, Hops shorter of breath but still strong enough to wrestle Carney to the ground if he had to, and at the top of the stairs, Hops takes a needed break while Carney wrangles with the mattress.

"Okay, okay," Hops capitulates wholeheartedly. "I just want to remind you that you have a godfather that cares."

That's a fact Carney doesn't need any reminding of; his godfather has been there for him in more ways than his own father. Still, Carney's in a difficult position. Hops always tells him the cold hard truth, but Carney just expected Hops would have more empathy. He and his late-wife, Betsy, Carney's godmother, were do-gooders themselves.

As they start down with the mattress, Carney tries to explain. "This girl," he says, getting lost as to how to describe a rare bird to a non-birdwatcher, "some people just live a story instead of imagining one." He trusts his eyes tell Hops how captivated he is by her. "I'm telling you, I feel like I'm supposed to rescue her," he says with conviction as they set the mattress on the boxspring. "I'm feeling something I haven't felt before. I'm inspired." He stands firm.

Hops gives him the ol' Gardner stare, the one he so famously gave the antihero in *Walking Alone*, along with countless other films, and grumbles, "I think lust and guilt have taken control of your brain. I'll keep my phone off silent 'til the Carney I recognize returns."

Carney laughs and tells him, "You do that."

Then Hops meanders over to the two boxes of items Carney ordered over Amazon: an accessible toilet chair, shower chair and bars. "Okay, now where's your Phillips?"

"My what?" Carney replies as he grabs a fresh pair of sheets from the closet. He wouldn't know a Phillips from a socket wrench. As an actor's son, that's just not how he was brought up. His dad didn't start his acting career while working in construction like Hops. Carney's dad was a bartender at a swanky country club, and besides that, he was rarely home to help fix anything anyhow. Even when he was home, he was memorizing his lines.

Hops raises his brow, silently judging his dead friend's parenting, and goes into the kitchen, flicks the light switch, nothing. He flicks it again. "How long has this been out?"

Carney knows he's usually on top of things, like dates, times, and light bulbs. Lately, the small details in his essential daily living have been hijacked by his escalating need for something more. He can't even pinpoint what it is that he needs, although he's betting it's whatever this girl has to bring to him, and he can't even remember when this need for something more or something different crept upon him. But the light bulb is pure evidence that it's been brewing for some time. So he meanders back into the kitchen.

"I don't know. A while," Carney mumbles, eyeing a nondescript aged wooden case that Hops placed on his kitchen counter when he arrived earlier.

Hops shakes his head and retorts, "You're lucky I'm handy," and then searches through the junk drawer for the tool he didn't think he'd have to bring with him.

"What's in this case you brought?" Carney hovers over the case with a polarizing curiosity.

Hops comes over to him with a Phillips screwdriver. "This is a Phillips, knucklehead."

Carney recognizes it right away. "Why didn't you say so?"

Hops laughs and says, "Open it," gesturing to the case and watches as Carney eagerly opens it revealing a shiny blued-steel Colt Army Revolver. "Your dad's gun from *Walking Alone*," Hops professes proudly. "Your pops killed a lot of bad guys with that Colt."

Carney holds it up with reminiscence thinking back to the day he worked with his dad on *Walking Alone*. In between camera setups, his father flicked open the loading gate with the expertise of an Old West sheriff and rolled the chamber to show him the bullets.

"These are blanks, of course," his dad said, "but this baby's real alright. Isn't she a beast?" His dad liked to refer to his cars, boats, and guns as women. Then his dad said, "This next set up is going to be your closeup. Just stay on my eyes and feel your reaction. You are this boy, and this boy is you." His dad stared into his eyes, telling him, "The closeup is the truth, everything is visible," and then showed a proud smile, patting him on the back like one of the boys. It was one of Carney's favorite memories. Then his acne arrived and his father's support for his acting career suddenly vanished. He remembers the night it happened, but the reflection of his scars on the gun frame brings him back to reality.

"Thanks, Hops. I'll treasure it," Carney says with his deepest sincerity. While Hops goes back to being handy, Carney remembers back to the night it happened.

It was after the divorce when his dad had just returned from a six-month overseas shoot. His dad called him up to meet for dinner at Micelli's, on Las Palmas Avenue. He had a surprise for his son. Carney just got his driver's license but took a cab because he didn't have a car. His car was waiting for him at the restaurant—the sparkling Chevy Nova that Carney now has in his garage. Mitch starred with the vehicle in his latest box office success at the time, called *Wild Ride*. But the real surprise wasn't just the car. It was a supporting lead in a Vietnam War film playing the younger brother who holds a family together after torn from loss.

Mitch was in a corner booth sitting with the famed producer, Connie Hawke, who had been following Carney since his first role in *Walking Alone*. She adored him in *Skateboard Heaven*, made just a few years after, but all that Carney found out through the course of the dinner. However, it was the look on his father's face when he first walked up, revealing his face full of acne that will be burned in his mind forever. Dinner didn't last long, and either did Carney's acting career. Once a week until his twenties, he would go to a dermatologist to have his cysts drained in the most barbaric way. He wasn't the same actor inside his head. He was scarred by then.

At least, his memory is still strong. He checks the chamber the way his father showed him how. The chamber's empty. But he knows where there's a gun store nearby.

CHAPTER NINE

Carney slides his credit card into the parking garage meter through his open car window, and the gate lifts. His Nova sparkles with nostalgia as he motors out of the structure and into the sunlight. Looking at his reflection in the rearview mirror—for sometimes the natural light complements the scars on his face—he tries to see the best in his appearance before swinging around to pick Pru up. He needs to be his best today. She needs him to be. Filled with purpose and a plan, he drives, imagining he looks like Steve McQueen in *Bullitt;* the hero inside himself is coming to life.

After two surgeries and almost a week in the hospital and playing about a million games of gin rummy, Pru's finally ready to come home with him. He still doesn't know her backstory, though, and every time he attempted to broach the subject of where she came from and how she was raised, she would click the button for the nurse to bring her more drugs. A sliver of an opportunity arose on Halloween when he came in wearing a pilot's uniform, and it got her excited. Her mood was so bubbly she opened up without him even having to ask.

She told him, "The only other Halloween I missed dressing up for was when I was locked up in juvenile hall."

That got his attention. Pru went on to explain that when she was fifteen, she stole her parents' car and ran away for a few days with her boyfriend. And when a cop tried to pull them over for speeding, her boyfriend didn't stop. He sped up instead and made quick right turns until he crashed her parents' car into a tree at a dead-end and ran, leaving her there to fend for herself with the cops. An early lesson to her that men only look out for themselves. Carney assured her that he would never do that to her.

When he got home that night, he took that nugget of a story to the bank, a 1940s bank, and built a backstory in his head for his main character that it was love that got her into crime and a man's disloyalty that made her split town. It explains how she became a thief. Not only did a man give her the idea, but he told her how to do it. If Carney had Pru's entire story, he'd be able to write a whole lot more, but he'll settle for what she's willing to give, for the moment.

He screeches to a halt in front of the hospital. Then, exiting the car, he walks tall, like his father in *Walking Alone*, toward the sliding doors to fetch his damsel in distress. Just inside, he finds her there waiting for him, sitting in a wheelchair with her discharge papers in hand, wearing the clothes he brought for her, his Cryptid Animal's t-shirt, and a pair of boxer shorts. The nurse hands him the hospital issued walker, which he balances over his shoulder before taking control of the wheelchair. He's prepared for this role. Like an actor rehearsing for a scene, he's visualized this jaunt to the car and everything that could go wrong. Her bandaged leg is extended out, and any bump would be excruciatingly painful, so he wheels her slowly toward the door, motioning for people to get out of the way. Then he pushes the handicap button to activate the sliding doors, and out they go.

Even though she's been freshly medicated and slightly dulled, she's excited to ride in the Nova. She briefly saw his car before they went on the motorcycle ride, but she never got a chance to admire it. Locking the wheels on the wheelchair, he opens the passenger door and snaps open the walker. The concerning part for him is that she has to pivot on her healthy leg to get in, and there is no preparation he can do; this is all on her. So he holds firm on the chair and the car door. Only she's so eager she practically hops in, like how she threw herself off of the bike after the accident.

"I bet she drives like a beaut!" she exclaims, loving his car.

Relieved that she's safe in the vehicle, he closes the door, folds up the walker, and puts it in the trunk, taking a momentary sigh of relief before sliding into the driver's seat, embodying his McQueen persona, hoping she's more than impressed by her hero.

But instead of thanking him for her rescue, she says, "I used to street race a '64 Mustang in the quarter-mile. Maybe you'll let me drive her one day?"

Another piece of her past, he praises. But refrains from asking her when or with who because he's learned it only quiets her up. So he revs the engine, vibrating her and the car.

"Spoken just like my dad," he mumbles from under his breath.

"Oh yeah?" she emits while strapping herself in.

"All our cars were female," he explains, "except for my mom's Monte Carlo. My dad would say, 'You can drive *him*. We'll be going in *her*,' pointing to his Porsche."

She laughs. "Well, of course."

Carney presses the gas gently, but his car is not built to drive slow. It wobbles and bobs over the hospital speed bumps like a boat. Seeing her brace for pain, he's concerned.

"She rides a lot smoother with speed," he advises.

"Then pedal to the gas, Romeo."

He's amused, wondering if she knows the saying is actually pedal to the metal. Then he hits the gas pedal, sending them flying down the main road that leads out of the hospital grounds, slowing to make a right on Wilshire before getting on Highway 405 South. The Nova is smooth. Pru sways back and forth slightly while holding strong onto the door handle. He weaves around cars to maintain speed, even while merging onto Interstate 10 West. That's when she lets go of her grip, not because she's relaxed, more like an astronaut when they first experience weightlessness. He wonders if it's because she trusts him or that she enjoys the danger. He settles on maybe it's both and takes the 4th Street exit to Main.

His hand is loose on the wheel as the Nova rumbles the speed limit down Main Street in Venice Beach. Windows are down, and the ocean breeze feels like freedom on her face. Carney maintains his calm, heroic mindset until he turns right onto Rose when sudden panic hits him like a tsunami wave. He hopes that he made the right choice and that the chore of it all will not suffocate their ability to get to know each other, and by that, he means his ability to get to know her. Switching hands on the wheel, he rubs out the sweat in his palm. She can tell his nerves are on edge, but all she can do for him is to be an excellent patient, which for the moment, means a cheerful disposition. She doesn't plan on needing much. Her schedule is pretty simple: sleep, eat, and take her medicine. The latter being her top priority.

After pulling into his garage, he helps her out of the car and inside his house. He points out the half-bath in the hallway with the handicap accessory installed just for her. In the living room, he points out the obvious that it's her bed there in the center of the room. With his nerves still on edge, he watches her hobble in with the walker, one hop at a time.

"Smells like vanilla," she says.

Feeling embarrassed, he admits, "I did that for you," and follows her with caution, realizing this is the longest she's been on foot.

"You didn't have to," she admits sweetly. Looking around, she notices there are no more ashtrays and can't believe all that he's done for her. She bathes in the light streaming in through the Venetian blinds and knows this is far better than she deserves.

"How will I ever repay you?"

He can't answer her nonsense at the moment, he's a wreck, and he'll feel a whole lot better once she gets her leg up.

"Here," he says with his hand delicately touching her back. "Let's get you lying down."

"That's what he said," she jokes.

He barely laughs, nervous, until she's sitting on the bed, and her leg is up on a pillow. Then he helps by propping up more pillows like a nest around not only her leg but her whole body. "I bought lots of pillows," he states the obvious, carefully and awkwardly stacking more and more pillows.

She looks like she just fell into a pile of marshmallows. It would be funny to Carney if he were in a lighter mood. He's not there yet. Although sitting down on the couch beside her bed, he feels the anxiety begin to alleviate.

She looks at him longingly. "Carney?"

"Yeah?" he calls back.

"I have to go to the bathroom," she says.

He puts on a good face, so she doesn't see how overwhelmed he feels already. "Okay, that was a good practice run. Here we go," he replies and removes the pillows one at a time until she's ready to stand up. She swings her leg around to stand, and he tries to help her with the walker.

"I got it," she insists with a smile, wanting to show him how capable she is, so he doesn't regret this. She stands with the walker, and he gives her room to find her way to the bathroom through streaks of sunlight. Then he follows her at a close distance like a protective angel, and, as the bathroom door closes, he takes a deep breath, free from responsibility.

Walking achingly out to the patio for a moment of clarity, he realizes he should be more than prepared for the emotional burdens of being a caregiver. His mother really put him through it at the end of her life, yelling at him as if he were his father. Angry because Carney reminded her so much of Mitch, the love of her life who cheated on her repeatedly. That's when Carney became aware that love is synonymous with hate. But he played it cool, letting his mom's hostility bounce off of him without making an imprint, and he nurtured her until the bitter end.

So why does Pru make him uneasy? She is practically a stranger, but he can't help his desire to help her. *Hell,* he admits to himself, *to be with her.* He would have never asked her to stay before the accident. She's a dangerous woman, after all. But he figures she can't possibly get into too much trouble, being injured.

Looking out at the boardwalk from his patio, he takes in his surroundings from a different perspective. Seeing the stark reality of the endless row of homeless tents, he can't believe how blind he's been, blind to the real issues in the world. *DING!* goes his phone.

He looks to see who's texting him. Danny O'Brien. His text reads, "HEY man, where the hell are you? You ignoring us? Maybe I have to come down there and drag your ass back here."

He can't let that happen to her, fresh from the hospital to be bombarded by company. No way. Plus, Danny has no idea what he'd be walking into; Carney hasn't told him or any of his friends. In fact, he's never gone MIA on them this long before unless he was working on a project. He wonders if maybe he should've told them about her but justifies that he wasn't in the right frame of mind to divulge the accident to anyone except Hops.

He texts back, "Hang tight. I'll be down in a bit."

He looks out at the horizon, wondering how his friends will take the news of her. Especially since telling Hops didn't go as well as planned. He should expect similar skepticism.

"Everything okay?" she asks from the patio door, seeing his troubled expression.

"Friends from Hemingway's," he replies back, in a momentary lapse, and then suddenly remembers he's nursing a sick bird. "What are you doing? We need to get your leg up." He ushers her back to her bed, and the propping of pillows continues again.

"What's Hemingway's?" she asks even though she already knows.

"A cigar bar I go to."

"Where everyone knows your name?" she jokes.

He looks at the clock on the tv box. 1:42PM. "You should take your pills before you start feeling anything," he asserts and goes to the pharmacy bag of medication he picked up the day before.

"I'll need food, even though I'm not really hungry."

"Okay, I have to go out anyway. I have some strawberries and bagels for now, but text me what you want."

"Text with what?"

"Oh shit, that's right." He completely forgot about her phone with everything else he had to do, and now he'll have two stops to make. "I'll get you a new phone too. What's your number?"

"Now, you ask?" she says sultry, and he laughs, finding a piece of paper and pen for her to write it on. "So tell me about Hemingway's," she continues, "because I know you'll be stopping by there for a while."

"Not long."

She questions that with a look because she gathers from his mental state he's in worse shape than her, and he'll need some time to unwind before returning home.

As he sits beside her on the couch, waiting for her to finish writing her number, she wonders, "Did you tell them about me?"

"I told Hops."

She hands him her number, asking, "Who's Hops?"

"My godfather."

Of course, you have a godfather, she thinks to herself, *you have everything a normal civilized person would have.* Then she insists, "Tell me about your rebel pack."

"Hmm, rebel pack, that's not too far fetched," he admits.

"Sounds like you have a type," she teases, not forgetting what he said about her in Vegas.

"I do tend to associate with colorful characters."

"What color am I?" she asks seductively.

He smiles, thinking *red, red, red. Hot, fiery, passionate red!* It isn't until later when he's standing in line at the T-Mobile, that he thinks a supernova explosion of colors would be more accurate. Here he is trying to get her to open up more, and what happens? He's the one divulging details about his friends, or his rebel pack, as she calls them. Telling her about Diaz, his tatted dark-skinned Cuban friend, and how he helped get him a screenwriter for his autobiography about his hard time in prison and how that hardness separates him from the pack. Then he tells her of his pal Danny O'Brien, the actor, and his reckless ways that remind him of his father, but that Danny has had it rough. His entire line of patriarchy—brothers and uncles included—are all in prison. When he goes on vacation, he visits half of the Midwest penitentiaries. Then going on, he explains the project that Mark has Danny sewn into, for some unknown reason, and how Carney feels he has to be protective of his friend.

He thinks he told her more than he should. He should play more of a game with her, speak her language. He has a lot to learn from her method. Her edges, once bristly, now appear smooth and comforting, disarming him completely. She has this down to an art form. He realizes she may continue to dodge and evade telling him of her past, but he can still learn a lot from her like this, how she plays him.

After moving up in line, he instructs the sales agent that he wants the pinnacle of iPhones for "this number," handing over the one she gave him. The sales agent tells him that number is past due two months and cannot be restored until it is paid in full. Carney hands over his American Express and tells him to ring it all up. He figures it is the least he could do.

The sun hovers high as he walks the short distance from the cellphone shop to Hemingway's Cigar & Bar. As he opens the big barred door of his beloved smoke-filled watering hole, he already notices a change about himself. He used to feel a draw coming here, but now it's been replaced by her. He can't wait to get back, but he greets his brood and lights a cigar in what was his favorite sofa chair that they saved for him.

Smoke hangs heavy in the air as he's surrounded by his rebel pack of colorful characters with their assorted-sized sticks aflame waiting for answers. He tells them how they met in Vegas, all but for seeing her swipe the hundred dollar bill and vaguely addresses her vanishing act to a misleading fact. "She didn't give me her number at the end of the night." Then he tells them how he supposedly ran into her on the boardwalk and what subsequently happened to them on the motorcycle. And, after their mouths agape, how she'll be recovering at his house. "So no drive-bys," he insists.

Shocked expressions fall like dominos. Carney can tell by Danny's downward drooping eyes that he's feeling dejected. For, Danny thinks himself to be Carney's best pal, and Carney isn't reciprocating expectations. Rocco, however, supports with a passionate back slap.

Curious for their opinion on it, Carney circles back to the crash to tell them what she said after he took her helmet off. "This girl looks up at me and says, 'At least we're on even keel again.'" Then looks around for a response.

"Who even says that?" Danny shoots back with some heat. "What's that even mean?"

"She has this thing with luck," Carney explains.

Their young friend they call Millennial, who they tease for wearing an expensive watch when he only ever looks at his Samsung for everything, looks up from his phone. "The keel is an aft-structure of a sailboat," he recites from Google.

Sarcastically, Rocco says, "Thanks for that, Millennial."

Carney feels their judgment creeping in, so he adds, "She's unlike anyone I've ever met," so they understand.

Diaz jokes with a straight face, "That'll get you six months."

Some of the other guys laugh, but Danny is still upset and in disbelief. "I've never heard you talk like this."

Carney assures him, "Man, I can't even tell you. I almost died. She really almost died. What can I say?"

"Nothing," Rocco replies. "It's beautiful, brother. I can't wait to meet her."

Carney realizes he's in a different time zone than his friends right now, and staying any longer here will give him jet lag, so he takes the last puff of his cigar and puts it out. "I should get back," he mumbles, but the truth is he wants to get back to her.

As he gets up, the last friend of the Hemingway's rebel pack shows up in one of his many colorful jackets, and it's the same slick guy who Pru told to zip up his fly at the mansion party.

"What's up, Mark?" Carney says halfheartedly.

"What's up? What did I miss?" Mark says arrogantly and slides into Carney's seat like he's the new king.

Rocco replies, "A whole lot. We'll fill you in."

As they all turn their attention to Mark, to give him their best rendition of Carney's tale, Carney leaves Hemingway's with the pink bag containing Pru's new cellphone. Halfway down the block, something in his intuition triggers him to turn around. He boomerangs back with suspicion, looking through the Hemingway's window, and sure enough, he sees them laugh and mock him. Did he miss the signs, or is this a new phenomenon because of his disappearance? If not something new, he wonders how long he's missed the signals and what else escaped him.

CHAPTER TEN

It's been grayer than usual, for fall is inching closer to winter, and today the rain finally broke loose. Thick droplets pelt the empty Venice Beach boardwalk, the birds are nowhere to be seen, and the igloos of tarp tents flap in the wind. While the homeless underneath hold down their forts, Pru sits comfortably inside Carney's protective nest, or his palace of pillows, knowing she surely won't be blown away. Not today, anyway. They're happy in isolation, listening to the rain make beats like tribal music.

"Stick me, baby," Pru whispers, erotically.

"Don't make me laugh," Carney pleas, holding the needle of blood thinner close to her belly, and after regaining his focus, he sticks her.

"Ow."

"Oh, shit. Did I hurt you?"

She teases, "You poked me good. A little rough for our first time."

He half laughs at her little joke. He's not surprised she would use sex as a tool when she's in no position to wield it and grabs a new bandage roll and gauze pads, determined not to be drawn into her web.

"Give me your leg, pretty girl."

She carefully swings her left leg to him. He holds her heel and removes her leg brace, which locks her knee in a minimal bend to protect the internal artistry done in surgery.

"I'm far from pretty right now," she says, baiting for a compliment because she only thinks of herself as pretty when she's in full hair and makeup.

He starts unwrapping the Ace bandage and says with all seriousness, "You could never know what ugly feels like." But that's not true. Pru has seen the ugly ruthless side of herself, which is the very thing she doesn't want him to know.

As she watches him unwrap the bandage, she's anxious to see the wreckage that's left. Only there is nothing to see because several gauze pads are stuck to her leg, covering her wounds and incisions. She observes as he carefully removes each one, revealing crusty scabby clusters and lines of staples, like zipper strips, where the surgeon made his incisions.

He explains, "This is where your leg broke and came through your skin," pointing at the large scabs.

Thankful she didn't look at her leg that day because she knows what broken bones look like under someone's loose skin, and it's an image from her past she can't numb herself from recalling, even though she has tried. So she forces herself from putting together the pieces as she navigates her wounds. But his pained expression tells her he's going into his memory bank and withdrawing those terrible images of her leg.

"It will be okay," she reassures him, "the body heals."

And like coming out of a trance, he places on fresh gauze pads and begins re-wrapping her leg with a new bandage, gaining assurance from her words. "I like that you're here," he acknowledges out-loud.

She doubts that's true. Although she believes that's what Carney thinks, for now, like lust that fades into hate, she feels so will his liking for having her here. His daily life has dramatically changed since the accident, and that's fine for now. She's the new shiny toy to play with until the toy becomes old, and from how quiet he was last night when he came home, she estimates his old toys have noticed.

"I bet your friends don't feel the same way," she says.

He sighs, wrapping past her knee, and mutters, "Friends are future enemies masquerading as allies." His depressive tone tells her all she needs to know.

"I see," she assesses right and hides a victorious smile. Victorious not because she doesn't want Carney to have friends, but because she wants priority over them. She wants to be Carney's top advisor, the one he vents to first, and the one he laughs with most. She opens her legs inviting him to wrap higher. And he does, holding hostage in his mind his thoughts of her inner thighs, how supple and smooth, and how untouched from the accident. He puts her brace back on, and she relaxes her leg back on her nest of pillows.

As he takes her old gauze pads to the kitchen trash, she estimates that things are going too smoothly and that it will quickly go the other way—that's what she does. So she looks for ways to rectify the situation and balance the tides. She tries fluffing up her hair, but it's so stringy and oily, and figures she can't possibly be attractive in this state. Then she smells her armpits and feels silly for flirting.

"I drink it black," he says, coming out from the kitchen with two filled coffee cups.

"Champagne or water, that's all I drink," she reminds him, doing her best to say it with a sweet tone, so it doesn't come across as bitchy, because she's too gross to pull off bitchy.

"You were serious?" he laughs off.

"I don't lie," she insists with seriousness in her tone because she dislikes when she's not believed.

Thinking it's like a game, he plays on, saying, "Just take a sip."

Just take a sip? She knows that game and believes all men learned this trick in their youth. "I've had coffee before," she scoffs. "I know what it tastes like."

He wonders if he's seeing a prima donna side to her. And if it's any match for him. He holds out a mug for her. "Taste is only a part of it. Who you drink it with is everything," he croons.

How can she deny him that? He wants to enjoy the moment with her. It'll make him happy. "Black it is," she says and takes the mug.

He smiles victoriously and sits next to her on the neighboring couch, sipping while ogling over her presence.

She wonders where he would regularly sit drinking his morning coffee? Would it be facing the television, or at the big table by the window? Maybe at the kitchen table or out on the patio. But the way he's facing her, it's like she's become his television or his ocean view. She takes a sip, and he watches for her reaction. She puts on a smile and plays the part. "*Mmmm*, to die for."

He laughs, appreciating the effort, and they sip in unison. It reminds him of watching his parents' morning routine when things were good between them, realizing he longed for a relationship with that kind of togetherness, where they can discuss the day's objectives and work together on the same goal. He doubts Pru will be that for him in the long-run, but that doesn't mean he can't play house with her in the meantime until they both get what they need.

"So other than Home Health coming by later to check on you, what do you want to do today?" he asks. "We can watch a movie, play gin rummy?"

She warns him, "You shouldn't treat me so nice. I may never leave."

He sips his coffee, imagining the 1940's story-version of Pru in his screenplay and where she would go next, when Pru blurts out, "What I really need is to take a shower."

Picturing her naked, he almost spits up his coffee. "We can do that," he says. Then, concerned he comes off too eager, he rolls it back, "How do we do that?" Then realizes, "I know how, they told me how," fumbling over his words, "but I mean, you're comfortable with that?"

She figures she's been nude in front of plenty of strangers before, so what's the difference?

Even though she's supposed to shower her leg without bandages, they both agree not this time. This shower will be a test run. She'll feel a lot safer with her leg brace on, anyway. So he covers her leg with a black garbage bag and tapes it around at the top, getting a good feel of her thighs. *Hold those thoughts,* he tells himself and guides her into his giant bedroom. Looking at his king-size four-post bed, she longs for the day she'll sleep there, but from the cord of his cellphone charger on the left side of the bed, she can tell he sleeps on the left. Her injured leg being the left one, she gathers that it may take a while before that happens.

Into his master bathroom, she understands why she's showering in here. He has a large granite walk-in shower with handles, and he's got a handicap shower chair there ready for her. He's prepared for everything, shampoo, conditioner, and body soap all within reach of the chair.

He stands there waiting for her to undress, and suddenly she feels uncharacteristically nervous. "On the spot, without all the glitz and glamour that seduction provides. Naked before I'm naked. I'm suddenly shy," she voices out-loud, in a rare moment of vulnerability.

He's amused. "My very own poem."

"This is hardly romantic."

"I have an idea."

She stands there with her walker balancing on one leg while he gets tea-light candles from under the sink and sets them up around the room. Looking up at the rain pounding down on the skylight above, she wonders why she feels so nervous. Then realizes what it is, whenever she's taken off her clothes for a man, she had the power; she orchestrated every *ooh* and *ahh*, but this is something else entirely. She's in unknown territory, and that makes her vulnerable. As he switches off the light, the room flickers with romance, and her very own Romeo stands before her, seeking her approval for this romantic gesture. That's when it comes to her, how to gain control and regain her strength.

"Lovely," she compliments, "but it doesn't seem fair. You get to see me, and I don't get to see you."

He ruminates over what she's subtly suggesting and figures she's already overlooked his facial scars. Why would his scarred chest be any different? He pulls off his shirt and explains with a pained remembrance, "My cystic acne was severe. It was on my chest and back, too."

"It doesn't look that bad," she says, wanting to touch him.

"You don't want to see what I looked like in high school. I always wanted to be an career actor like my pops, but then I got this," he confesses, easing into her gaze.

She watches him fully undress. "I think you're sexy," she smiles victorious, looking at his naked body.

He goes to her, emphasizing the sincerity in his voice, "No, *you're* sexy. And beautiful."

Looking into his eyes, she'd like to believe that he sees inside her soul and thinks she's beautiful on the inside too. Even though she knows it's dark in there, and too many cobwebs lie around, but maybe he could hang lights and clear away the pieces of her past. She tells herself not to get too excited and wakes herself up from the fantasy.

"Hold my waist," she instructs.

He wraps his large hands around her tiny waist, keeping her balanced while she lets go of the walker, freeing her hands to peel off her shirt, tossing it onto the floor. She hasn't had a bra since the accident. They cut off all her clothes at the hospital, so she stands topless with full use of her arms. He has to hold himself back from ogling over the beauty of her breasts.

Taking full advantage of her mobility, she caresses his chest, ignoring the scars. He has the build of a Greek god, an Olympian, and from the bar in his closet doorway, she can tell he does plenty of pull-ups. She longs to feel him skin to skin and imagines what he'd feel like inside her.

She says softly, "This is just about the longest second date of my life."

"You got that right."

Their lips magnetically attract into a kiss. It feels natural, the passion igniting like a fuse. Pru caressingly feels his chest and shoulders, and as the kiss heats up, he wants to caress her body, only there's nowhere for the passion to progress onward as she struggles with all her weight on only her one sturdy leg. They figure perhaps it's the reminder they needed.

"Shower?" she sighs.

"Shower," he agrees.

With romance out the window, she readies herself. Using her walker to position herself in front of the large glass shower door, he opens it.

"Okay, pretty girl, boxers down, pivot and sit."

With one free hand, she awkwardly pulls down the boxers to her knees. Carney gives her a sturdy arm for support so she can lean back blindly onto the chair, she bobbles a bit, but he holds her steady.

"You okay?"

"Good," she nods, sitting side-saddle on the shower chair. "Can you?" she asks, referring to the boxers, and he slides them over her ankles, doing his best to be respectful and keep eye contact. She sees his struggle and starts laughing, so he laughs too, easing the stress of the situation.

"Ready?" he asks, and she nods.

She swivels her uninjured leg onto the shower floor, and he helps guide the injured one forward. She is safe inside. He prepares the water masterfully, balancing the cold and hot dials just right, and closes the door to let her shower.

She lets the water wash over her, washing away the stress and anxiety, and for a moment, she feels like her old self, in mind only, and moans orgasmically, "Oh my god, this feels amazing!"

He puts on his boxers, hiding his arousal. "I'm going to get you some fresh clothes," he says, his arousal hindering his steps forward. He heads into his bedroom and beelines for his boxer drawer. Suddenly he wonders if he'll have to share his boxers with her everyday. He brought her clothes for her hospital release because she needed comfy clothes to be released in. But it occurs to him that she must have clothes somewhere, probably sitting in a bag beside someone's couch.

"Where are your clothes?" he yells to her.

"In my car!"

"Where is your car?"

"Down the street," she shouts, but as soon as she said it, she wished she could take it back.

CHAPTER ELEVEN

Carney hangs his jacket over his head, shielding himself from the rain. He steps quickly through puddles, pressing Pru's car key clicker repeatedly, listening, through the sound of raindrops smacking the wet pavement, for her white car to identify itself. Then he hears *a beep, beep,* and looks. The beat-up sedan's dim taillights signal a distress call, so he crosses the street and peels off two soaking wet parking tickets from its windshield before getting inside.

The smell is musty like an old closet, and from the looks of it, the bags of clothes and shoeboxes, it is a closet, evidence that she lives out of her car. He imagines her lifestyle and that she must feel discombobulated, not knowing where everything is or where she is.

The sound of the rain thumping down on the car around him makes him feel closed in, and uncomfortable feelings rise to the surface. Wondering what mysteries lay hidden here, he opens the glove compartment and out pops a taser gun among stacks of paper and the vehicle's manual. The taser gun doesn't surprise him. He puts it back and grabs her car registration, not knowing if it will verify key-details, and there it is. He reads, "Ruby

Prudencia Romiti," just like he saw at the hospital, and there's a Los Angeles address. He pulls out his phone, opens up Maps, and types in the address as he sees it, zooming in on the street view only to see that it's a shipping business. He presumes they rent post boxes, and that's how she maintains an address. Hiring a private investigator comes to mind, but then he remembers her concern about him being one, so he thinks again. Maybe she has reasons for being off-grid. Whoever might be looking for her doesn't need to find her because he made the stupid mistake of getting another person involved in unraveling her mystery. He's only feeling the need to do this because his patience is paper-thin and he's craving more information.

He puts her registration back and starts the car. Pulling out of the space, he wonders, what are the odds that she happened to park that close, could be cosmic, or then again.

Removing the garage remote from his pocket, he presses the button. It opens, and he pulls into the empty space where his motorcycle would be if it weren't at the repair shop. Standing at the garage door to enter the house with a few of her bags, he looks at the two vehicles, his shiny black Nova and her beat-up white sedan. They are visual representations of the two of them. One is aged yet well looked after. The other is overused and easily seen as a stain to society.

Coming inside, he drops her things behind the couch by the living room wall. "You were parked really close," he says to her before going to the kitchen to dry off his face with a paper towel and remove his jacket. Expecting grand approval, he adds, "There were a couple of parking tickets, nothing I can't handle," but she doesn't reply. He walks over to her bed, where he left her, and finds her out like a light, tucked in, and leg up.

He stares at her, trying to understand. No one lives that way unless their options are diminished or pure willpower prevents them from living a life of responsibility. Drug addict? He wonders for a moment before acknowledging that he would've noticed her going through symptoms of withdrawal. He figures maybe she's running from something or someone and gathers ideas for his story. That she ran away from a sinister man, perhaps it was this man's idea to rob the bank, and he'll eventually be coming for what's his. And this man would do anything to find her. She'll have to change her appearance and change her direction.

Carney walks over to the table by the window and opens up his laptop. Retrieving his file from his email labeled "Untitled Pru Story," he sets his cursor in the right spot to start typing.

Meanwhile, Pru pretends to sleep, avoiding the situation. Embarrassed by what her car says about the state of her life, she doesn't want to be in the position of having to justify her means of existence, but there's no other way to speak of it without having to explain herself. It's not something to be proud of, and yet she knows what led her down that path, and that's not something she feels comfortable disclosing as of now. There's a million different ways the conversation could go, and she can't afford half of them. Causing a rift with the man who holds her future in her hands is a sure means to an end. But how long can she go on like this, not talking about her past? She peeks through her eyelashes at him while he looks at his computer screen, typing away with an image of her in his head.

INT. (1940'S) THRIFTY'S DRUGSTORE - LOS ANGELES - DAY

She knew she needed to start a new life, so she grabbed the Clairol hair dye from the counter.

INT. (1940'S) HOTEL ROOM - DAY

Shower steam fills the hotel room as the red dye runs down her shapely body.

NARRATOR (V.O.)
Mexico was on her mind, and Penny would be her new name.

While he's typing, he whispers the Narrator's line. "Mexico was on her mind, and Penny would be her new name."

Pru tries not to smile.

CHAPTER TWELVE

Pru's been trying not to smile all week, concerned she'll tip the scales too far into happiness, and it will all swing back the other way. So she remains pleasant and delightful, but Carney's been so wonderful, it's hard for her not to enjoy it here and enjoy him. She could easily get situated to life in Venice Beach with him, might even see herself with a job, and being satisfied with the banal, simplicity of things. Life could be decent and possibly joyful, she thinks, as she sits comfortably at the big table by the window with her leg up looking outside, her hair brushed and makeup applied. But an inkling of doubt reigns overhead, an omen of death like she's seen a black butterfly. Only there are no omens or symbols. It's all in her head.

The thick gray marine layer hovers lower than usual over the calm ocean. The beaches are nearly empty of tourists. She watches the birds out the window hunt for food around Carney's patio, her favorite pastime this week. It's been a while since she could enjoy her surroundings so peacefully. She focuses on the same glossy blackbird as the days before. Its round belly, small beak, and pale eyes differentiate it from the proud raven, though it's doing a good impression. She can almost relate. She wonders if the glossy blackbird mated with a raven; would that make it a raven too? Or would she always be seen as different, an imitation? Carney finishes injecting her daily shot of blood thinner into her abdomen so stealthily she hardly notices.

"You're getting pretty good at that, Romeo," she says before taking a sip of coffee.

"Just as I don't need to do it anymore," he says, with a hint of sadness for the passing of time. Then takes a seat at the table for his favorite time of the day, their coffee hour. The only thing that would make it better is if she were to open up about her past. He's been loading on the kindness all week and hinting that he'd like to know more about her. If she weren't also so easygoing, he might have had to be more forceful about it. Although, he never expected she wouldn't even ask a single question about his dad. Or what it was like to grow up as his son. And he has to admit that it's refreshing. He can just be with her and share the same air, comfortably as if they've been doing it for years.

"I wonder what life will be like after I heal. Where will I be?" she asks subtly, testing the waters.

He doesn't have the answer for her. The future is a strange mistress he's learned not to dream of, for she only disappoints. *Ding!* goes his phone, and he looks at the notification to see who's texting: Millennial. It reads, "Hey man got something for ya. Meet me at HCB." Carney knows HCB is Millennial speak for Hemingway's Cigar & Bar, but he has no idea what he's got for him, and he doesn't care. He ignores it without opening the message, puts his phone back in his pocket, goes back to sipping his coffee, and people watching outside. On the boardwalk, the homeless woman with two long braids rearranges her trash, or what she might call possessions, within a shopping cart. He wonders if this vision is what Pru has in her mind as she wonders about her future. The comfortable silence suddenly closes in on him like a vice. He feels pressure to tell her that she'll be all right, but if he could predict the future, he wouldn't be so lost himself. His phone dings again, alerting him of the unread message. It means nothing to him. She's got his full attention. Thinking back to her car that she uses for a closet and the conversation they never had, he has many questions he's sure she'll never answer. But he's got to do something to release the pressure, so he asks anyway.

"I'm curious, how does one vagabond these days? Is it still as magical as the '60s implied, or are you a repo away from living in a tent?"

She reads his judgment clear as day and realizes that the glossy blackbird outside could never mate with a raven nor assimilate with a raven life. She'll always be seen for who she's been, an imitation. Her past will live in the present, like a false reality haunting her for the remainder of her days.

"I see," she states, matter-of-factly, accepting the bleak view of her future so that it doesn't suffocate her from within.

"What?" he wonders.

She sips her coffee, but a sudden distaste overwhelms her enjoyment of it. She'd prefer to leave the conversation there, but she feels forced to explain herself, so she snaps, "It's so typical. I don't know why I'm so surprised. It was bound to happen."

"No, I really want to know," he says, trying to guide her back to a place where she could open up.

"No, you don't," she resists. "You want to know you're not with some psycho who'll transform in front of your eyes."

His eyes widen. "Oh, I know I'm with a psycho. I only hope to never make you angry enough to show me."

She laughs.

He switches gears. "I don't *really* think you're a psycho," he says earnestly. "I know how easily any woman can be pushed to that point."

She knows all too well the truth in that. There is no telling the depth of her darkness if she's pushed. And she's comforted by Carney's acknowledgment of it. So often, it goes the other way. He keeps surprising her.

"So you just want to know, no judgment?" she asks.

He'd have to be from another planet to promise something like that. Judgment is human nature, so he pleas, "Define judgment."

She clarifies, "Deal breaking assumptions."

He agrees, "In that case, yes. No judgment."

She knows that if she tells him how she deals with life living couch to couch, that would be letting him in on how she thinks on *his* couch, so to speak, bringing light to a hidden side of her, a side of herself she's never shown anyone before. A precarious situation for her, but he agreed to no judgment. All she can do is take him at his word, so she decides this is more of a test for him.

Taking her time, much like an actress on a stage, she finds the truth within. "It's not magical," she elucidates, "every day there are objectives and negotiations. Some days are easier than others, and some days don't even belong to yourself. That's the cost of singing for your supper. And the days that mold you or refine you down to who you really are—when you have to make a decision that determines your morals—those days I like the most, in retrospect. There's strength in that, controlling your future when so much of your life is going with the wind." She looks at him, gauging his reaction.

"I like the way you talk," he smiles at her like she's his character come to life. Ideas are flowing through his mind. "How do I keep you talking?"

She relaxes into the reflection of herself on his face and turns heavy on the seduction dial. "It's simple, put a quarter in the meter."

"Why are you so quick to go to sex?" he asks, striking a nerve in her, and it shows.

Her defenses go back up. "We all use what we've been given."

"But there's so much more to you than that," he urges her to see.

"You'd be the only one alive who's said that to me," she affirms with a touch of sadness in her eyes.

He's confused by that but really wants to know. "Why don't you want to see yourself in a better light?"

"I don't have time," she says, guarding herself. "You want to know the difference between me and the homeless out there?" She gestures outside toward the homeless woman. "It's hard to dust yourself off again and again as if all that pain never existed and look at humanity with hope and trust. I do that work every day. Despite what I've been through, I try. I don't give up." She moves her leg off the pillows and hastily grabs for her walker, wanting to escape.

He gets off his chair, nervous for her. "Whoa. You can't fly away this time. You've got nowhere to go."

She indeed has nowhere to go, so she sits back, relinquishing the fight. She's always welcome back at the dilapidated mansion in the Hollywood Hills, but an injury is not sexy. It would only be a matter of time before her invitation expired. This is not only the one place she has, but it's also the only place she wants to be.

She plays a different hand, playfully saying, "I'm like a helpless pet. You feed me, bathe me..."

He interjects, "A pet wouldn't talk back."

She laughs.

He sits back down at the table, confident that the waters have been calmed. She melts away her defensive walls, easing into the feeling of being in his capable hands. Trust, it's a horrifying feeling. It scares her to rely on him like this, both physically and emotionally.

"If only you could promise me that everything would be all right, that you won't kick me out when I heal, that we are real, and that nothing will happen to you."

"Happen to me?" he spits out instinctually, needing to know what she means by that.

With an eerie tone, she voices, "The last three guys I dated died," and looks out the window as if she's looking somewhere in the past.

That sets him up straight.

"Come on, now," he urges her to be honest.

She looks at him with the coldest yet most hypnotic eyes he's ever seen. "I told you. I don't lie."

He fears he may have pushed her past that point, so he freezes, not wanting to stir the pot. She reads that he backed off so she softens.

"So often I'm not believed," she explains. "I want you to know that it's important you believe me."

He nods, still curious about what that means: the past three guys she dated died. Questions are flooding through his mind, and his blood pressure rises, wondering if she really is as dangerous as she seemed that day they met. His thoughts go back to when she told him her Vegas story and how unbelievable that sounded. He wonders if her truth is really the truth. Perhaps she lives in a reality of her own to protect the uncomfortable, embarrassing actuality underneath. That she makes a lot of poor choices and dates the wrong men, men who live so dangerously that they are more likely to die. He stands, feeling the weight of it.

"That's a hell of an ace to hold," he exclaims, pacing. He hopes she's a heck of an actress because if it really did happen, he's worried about his own safety. Going down the rabbit hole, he wonders if maybe someone is killing her boyfriends in a jealous, crazy rage. He could see that happening. He goes to the sliding glass door and scans the boardwalk for stalkers. "You have a crazy ex-lover or something I should know about?"

She hesitates and then says, "No," but then thinks maybe, but then decides, "no, definitely not."

His phone dings, making him flinch. He looks down at it. It's Millennial again, saying, "You coming?!"

He ignores it, again, for obvious reasons—she is finally opening up about her past. Needing to know more, he turns to her and asks, "How did they die?"

"I told you about Vegas," she locks eyes. "The guy after him had a heart attack, and the third was suicide."

He figures if it were actually a killer doing all this, he would have to be very talented to pull it off in all those scenarios. And if she's not involved somehow, or the catalyst, she just has some terrible luck. That's when it hits him.

"I see," he says, looking down at her.

"What?"

"You think it's your fault, this luck thing, pushing your luck like you have nothing but bad luck."

She partly admits it, "Maybe."

He continues, "You left me in Vegas because you thought your bad luck would kill me next?" He makes his way back to her at the table.

"I wish I could be that selfless," she acknowledges, shamefully. "I left because I needed the upper hand." She smiles, embracing the truth. "You seem like a guy that girls behave well around. They don't know you need something different."

"So, all I needed was you?"

She doesn't supply him with an answer. She just sits back with a confident, playful stare, daring him to play on to find out for himself.

He takes the opportunity to ask, "Where did you go? When you left me in the suite, where did you go? I don't envision you going back to your room and calling it a night."

She stares blankly. "I sobered up and people-watched, then drove back to L.A. Do you believe me?"

"I do," he says without hesitation, enjoying this game of theirs. He admits, "You're not boring, I'll give you that."

She looks back at him longingly, with hope for a future, but then says, “You’re not a bad guy to recover from a broken leg with.”

He laughs.

CHAPTER THIRTEEN

Even away from her, Carney can't resist Pru's pull. He sees her in his eyelids when he closes his eyes. She lives in all the crevasses of his brain. His motor reaction responds to her daily needs for food, shower, or changing her bandage. Every time he helps her into the shower, he craves her more, although her lips are as far south as he's traveled. She's his first thought in the morning and his last thought at night. He wonders if this is what a drug addict feels like, he wouldn't know, and he doesn't care to quit.

Inspired, he looks at life with new eyes, like he bought a new camera. He is viewing the world through a wider aperture, never having noticed before that the Santa Monica Community College is filled with so many vibrant colors. He can see things that he previously missed—the modern architecture and striking palms—even though he's been teaching here every Tuesday (Spring and Fall semesters) since his father died.

He enters the classroom of amateur filmmakers. Some are old, most are young, and sit scattered apart, only filling up half of the thirty-seat room. To Carney, they look more like a half-empty bleacher crowd ready to cheer on a hopeless team. Standing in front of his desk, he starts by explaining camera lenses. His students take notes enthusiastically for the first thirty minutes before noticing their energy waiver. So he throws in an example from *Walking Alone*, how the wide-angle captured his father walking across the vast desert to The Bagman, to the long lens that showed the deceitful expression The Bagman had on his face. A fury of notes drums on again, but they still don't understand how and when to use these lenses from a directorial standpoint, the professor's affliction, no one truly understands until they get their hands dirty.

Meanwhile, the beach house is bombarded by loud shouting coming from the tent inhabitants outside. Pru tries to block it from her consciousness, but that is a near impossibility. So she takes full advantage of her time alone to keep her mind off of the ruckus. Shuffling her walker over to the red EQ box on the floor, pulling the plastic bin toward her, and pops the top. Light dust glitters in the air as she leans the top against the side of the box. Inside, there's a flashlight, battery charger, batteries, AM Radio, and a first aid kit. No money like Carney insinuated. She returns the box to its place, giving a quick dusting, before shuffling off into his bedroom to snoop around in there.

Knowing men, she goes first to his sock drawer. Moving the top layer of socks back, she finds a pair of solid gold cufflinks. From the enlarged square and starburst projecting from a diamond, she figures they're from the '70s or '80s. She assumes they're inherited from his father and keeps digging, finding his checkbook and what looks like a safe deposit box key. Then she puts them all back and shuffles over to his nightstand, a chunky wooden piece that matches the chest of drawers and has fresh water-rings collecting dust. Finding a reason to be useful, she hobbles into his bathroom and finds cleaner and rags under the sink. She'll be able to do more of this when she has more mobility. For now, it's difficult for her to stay on one leg that long, but she can at least clean his nightstand for him before it stains permanently.

Back to snooping inside the nightstand, she finds a pot-pen on top of a weathered mystery novel, condoms, and body lotion. She takes a hit from the pen and closes the drawer, coughing a couple of times. It's been a while. Then she swipes her hand in between the mattress and the boxspring, feeling papers of some kind, and grabbing the stack of them, she pulls them out only to see that it is an old '80s Playboy. She wonders if Carney inherited not only his father's beach house but his life too. *No wonder he's depressed,* she says to herself. *He's trying to fill shoes that aren't his.*

She sees the old gun case Hops gave to Carney, next to his bed, and wonders what's inside. After picking it up by its thin brass handle, she lays the case flat on the bed to open it. She doesn't recognize the gun from the film, *Walking Alone.* All she sees is the menacing power of a gun, she's no stranger, but it's been years since she's handled one. She gives this Colt Army Revolver a once over before finding the release on the right side, flicks open the loading gate to see a shiny bullet sleeping in the visible chamber. *This gun is loaded.*

She places it in the canvas bag she tied to her walker and puts the gun case back where she found it before shuffling back to her bed to take a pain pill. The shouting outside has calmed to intense chatter and mad laughter, but Pru's nerves are still aflutter. Pulling the gun from her walker bag, she lays it on the floor within arm's reach. As she leans back into her pillows, the weed takes effect first. The sun sets, and so do her eyelids.

"We all see out of different lenses," Carney preaches to his class. "Sometimes, it's a wide-angle, and everything is in focus, and the world around your character is in focus too, sometimes for necessity." He refers back to the *Walking Alone* scene where the femme fatal stands behind his father, in focus, taking a gun from her purse.

"The closer your characters get to each other, the more intimate they get." He thinks about Pru. "The lens gets closer and more centralized, and the background becomes nonexistent, blurred." He walks among their desks, speaking passionately. "You can grow your lenses, first at 50 millimeters, then 75, to 200 millimeters, where the script should have your characters looking into their souls." The class stares back at him, attempting to feel his passion but have no idea. "That's just one example," he says, coming back from being lost in visuals of Pru and oscillates to the front of the class. "That's not to say there are any set rules, other than what works for that scene. Just keep in mind that going too far off common technique could throw your audience off. But maybe something is exciting in that, and best of luck to you, you'll be paving your own path." He looks at the clock. "Okay, that's all for tonight," he concludes, and immediately the students bustle their notes into their bags and shuffle out.

Pru's eyes dart under closed eyelids to the light of the television, her hand hangs over the bed, dead in the air, and the gun remains in its same place on the floor. The sounds of Carney entering don't wake her.

Ignoring his old routine of flicking on the kitchen light, he goes directly to her on the couch, seeing her sound asleep with the glow of the tv on her face. If he were looking, he could easily see the gun from there. But he's focused on only her, like a closeup, and the gun's not even in his shot. Then like a loving caretaker, he grabs the remote and turns off the fifty-five-inch screen.

Heading to his bedroom with his leather messenger bag, he flicks on the soft light from his nightstand. Gets undressed, slides into the sheets with his computer, takes a hit of his night medicine from his drawer and begins to write.

NARRATOR (V.O.)
She chose this bar because it was close to the docks.

INT. 1940'S SAN PEDRO BAR BY DOCKS - NIGHT

Prudencia as Penny enters the bar like a lioness, hunting.

NARRATOR (V.O.)
Surely she could count on a lonely sailor to believe her tale of woe and take her in.

She walks down the bar of beaten-down old men, searching.

NARRATOR (V.O.)
It's easy to spot the fisherman, their faces deeply lined and sunbaked, fingers calloused by nylon ropes and sea salt.

One Sea Salt drinking alone takes notice, the younger of the lot.

FISHERMAN
How ya doin', Angel?

PENNY
Buy me a drink, Captain?

FISHERMAN
I'm no captain.

PENNY
I'm no angel.

He waves to the bartender as she sidles up on a stool next to his.

FISHERMAN
That's good. This is no place for angels.

PENNY
Good. I'm having a devil of a time finding a place to stay the night.

Bartender delivers two shots, and the fisherman raises his—

FISHERMAN
To midnight drifters and devil's luck.

Pru suddenly awakes to see Carney's light on, so she reaches down in a panic to see if the gun is still there. Thankfully, it is! Quickly, she hides it under her mattress. Unable to go back to sleep, she turns on the tv, a luxury she hasn't had since childhood. Carney hears the familiar click and looks to see the hall illuminated with the glow of television light. He puts his computer aside and grabs his phone.

Her phone lights up with his name. She answers breathy and pleasant, "Hello there."

"Let me ask you a question," he speaks low and soft like it's a secret. "When you were a phone sex actress, how did that go?"

She's quick to realize, saying, "Oh, so this is one of those calls?"

"Well, maybe," he pauses to imagine before continuing on, "but seriously, I want to hear what that was like. Did you go right into it? How did you lure them in?"

"Well, all the calls were categorized by what you desire. Like college girl, redhead, big tits. And then the caller would let me know what they wanted." She breathes heavily into the phone, seductively purring, "So what do you want?"

Then another call tries to come through. When Carney sees it's a call from Millennial, he could not be more irritated. He dismisses him to voicemail.

"I want you," he divulges to her. "I've wanted you since the day we met."

She smiles devilishly, thinking back to that night. "You could've had me in the hallway after the concert."

Carney closes his eyes, imagining he was free enough to have no inhibitions. "How would that go?"

"You put me against the wall and kiss my neck," she moans, imagining. "And slide your hands up my thighs, lifting my dress."

He imagines doing everything she's saying.

"You're pleased to see I'm not wearing any underwear."

He cuts her off, "Were you really not wearing any underwear?"

She gives a sinister laugh, continuing, "You lift me up against the wall and kiss me. I wrap my legs around you. You want me as much as I want you. And we can't wait anymore. I unzip your pants, and..."

CHAPTER FOURTEEN

In this prodigious, modern medical center waiting room that looks more like a government building, Carney and Pru wait with her call number in hand for her orthopedic surgeon. Carney's nervous for her and tells himself her leg is obviously going through the stages of healing, although the swelling hasn't subsided, and according to her, the pain is increasing. Then a vibration in his pocket diverts his thoughts to his phone. It's a call from Danny. He lets her know he'll be a minute. She smiles, showing her patience, and he makes his way outside.

"Hey man, how's it going?" Carney asks his friend.

"Going good. Did you know Millennial has been trying to reach you?"

Carney feels a rush of guilt. "Ya. I meant to text him back. We've been busy."

"You should really call him back. He wants your help with this IP." Carney's familiar with IP, short for intellectual property, he acquired the book rights, or IP, for two of his films, *Corner of Love* and *Tiger in the Shallow.*

Danny emphasizes, "He's got Scott Manford attached."

Carney's shocked. "Scott Manford?"

It's been well over a decade since he last crossed paths with his old friend, Scott Manford. They were in their mid-twenties, and Scott was featured on Variety's Top 10 Rising Stars. Now his old friend is in high demand, filming three movies a year, with high profiled commercials spliced in-between.

Carney asks skeptically, "How in the world did Millennial bag Scott?"

"They ran into each other at the Emmy's. Like literally, Millennial was getting up from his seat just as Scott was coming down the aisle."

"What? Scott's not that easy of a grab." Carney scratches his head. "What's the IP? How did he get it?"

"Just give him a call."

Amid all the Thanksgiving decorations on the medical center window, Carney peers in to check on Pru.

"I don't know. I'm busy right now. I don't know if I have the time."

"Seriously?!" Danny says. "You've been struggling to get a project going for over a year, and suddenly you're busy! Just give him a call and hear him out."

Carney promises he will and hangs up the phone, but everything in him has no desire to hear him out. His mind has already closed the door to anything that isn't Pru, or his "Untitled Pru Story." As he comes back in to sit beside her, thoughts stream through his head. If he takes a shot on this, it will take him away from her. He figures, isn't that just how it goes? You get what you want just as you don't want it anymore.

The numbers tick on the call box on the wall, and he reaches out to hold her hand. He justifies that he couldn't commit himself to it; she needs him. Then he wonders why he's doing this to himself. It's like he's trying to reason himself out of it when Danny is right; he's been aching for a project.

She knows he's lost in his head after the call. He's staring into the air without any forbearance of current events. Even though his eyes appear to be fixed upon the call box, he doesn't flinch when their number comes up. She knows better than to ruffle the waters of his thoughts. He's doing so much for her already. She shouldn't demand that he give her all his thoughts too. Not yet anyway, she thinks to herself as she gently lets him know they're called.

After a good twenty minutes of x-rays, they find themselves in room number five, staring at the images of Pru's leg lit up on the wall. Metal rods, from her foot to her hip, and plenty of screws in between. He should feel reassured. The doctor says she's healing according to plan and shouldn't need any more pain pills. Great news, but inside his head, he struggles mightily with the memory of her crushed leg at the scene of the accident. Images of her bones protruding through her jeans flying through his mind like an avant-garde horror film. Feeling his energy, she squeezes his hand as the doctor sends in a young male nurse to pluck staples from her thigh. She moans with pain, but to Carney, it sounds erotic, and he knows he's not the only one who thinks so as the male nurse looks up from her leg.

Suddenly the thought occurs to him, w*hat if she lost the leg?* He tries to calm himself with the reminder that she didn't lose her leg and that maybe he saved it by keeping the bike up. He wants to feel like her hero, but he's having a hard time doing that today. There are too many thoughts racing around in his mind, and as the room's white walls close in on him, it brings him back to a terrible memory from his childhood when he was locked in a room and couldn't escape. He forces the daymare away, he hasn't eaten all day, and he had way too many cups of coffee. His skin feels ugly, and her near-fresh wounds of future scars remind him of his and the years of healing, hurting, and public scrutiny. Thinking of her beauty, her perfect beauty, now scarred forever, he aches for her and for himself. The guilt creeps up again like a poison slowly seeping into his system. He needs to get out of here, anywhere, somewhere. But he can't leave her, so he waits, patiently, until every staple is plucked from her leg and then wheels her back to the car.

One more stop to go, down the street to physical therapy where he'll wait some more. Pru doesn't need her wheelchair for this. Handicap parking gets them right upfront of the one-story building, an old strip mall that hasn't had a fresh coat of paint since the Clinton administration. The waiting room is smaller, and the elongated panels of floor to ceiling windows give the feeling of a cage. His leg revs up and down like a piston, ready to go when she's called. Until then, he stays by her side, his thoughts still swirling around in his head, forming a tornado. When the tornado finally makes landfall, he tells her what he thinks. "You're scarred like me now."

Although she doesn't see his scars and wonders if she'll ever get that way with herself, not seeing hers. Or will they always stare back at her with remembrance? For now, it's an indifferent remembrance, which is as best as she could be for going through such a traumatic situation. But she questions how it will be going forward without pain pills. She can't deny that she enjoys the emotion numbing from them. External scars are nothing compared to the mental torture that scars her from within.

"At least my outsides match my insides," she replies, hoping her realistic outlook will ease his pain. But from the way he strokes his scars with a fixed gaze, she can tell his internal torment might be ripping him apart inside, scarring like her now. She runs her hand through his pompadour and whispers declaratively, "This isn't your fault."

But her positive attitude isn't calming him down at all. He asks, "How can you be so good about this?"

Taking a quiet breath, she sees that clearly, her internal scars are far more severe. She is only able to be positive because there is nowhere else to go but up. She says, "No one skates through life without a few scars, physical or otherwise." But he can't even hear anything sane right now. His anger is ticking up like a bomb about to blow.

A handsome Hawaiian physical therapist steps forward and calls out, "Prudencia?"

Carney looks up at his flawless face. He's a pure specimen of a man with all the perfect male attributes. *How the fuck is this guy not in Central Casting for a Hawaiian hero role. Obviously, he's an actor with a physical therapy degree and occupation until the big break flows.*

Pru hesitates before rising, looking at Carney with concern.

He assures her, "I'll be here when you're done."

So she rises to her walker and shuffles over to the handsome man. Carney forces a smile and a nod to the therapist before high-tailing it out as fast as possible. She turns back to look at him, but he's halfway to his car, jingling his keys like he's free. Free from society's restraints, the composure demanded of him his entire life, and always looked at as Mitch McMorris' son. *You can't do that; you have to be this way*, ringing around in his head. Listening to his emotions has never been a luxury he could take advantage of.

His thoughts are on fire as the Nova roars in reverse. The rear wheels lock momentarily, and he jams the stick into drive. The engine rumbles, and the rear wheels spin fiercely forward, making a short high-pitched screech as he exits the parking lot.

On Wilshire Boulevard, his anger climbs into the red as his Nova shoots up in RPMs. It's as if he's chasing someone, maybe himself, unaware of how fast, concentrated on cars and street lights ahead of him. Following the road rules, he dodges around a slow car and halts on a dime, idling at a stoplight. *Way too many red lights in my life lately*, he thinks. His foot inches off the brake; he wants to bust through, the intersection is clear. He could do it if he wanted to. But being the son of Mitch McMorris, he waits dutifully until the light turns green, then he's off to the races.

Realizing he has no specific place to go, he's driving just to let off some steam, but he starts to get turned around, turning left to turn left, no particular reason why except to take a chance that the freeway is somewhere around here. Not feeling like himself, he wants to let loose and fly down the interstate. Searching, he takes another left and runs into a neighborhood dead end. *What the hell is going on*? He throws it into reverse and starts all over again.

He's getting used to the constant shifting of directions, but the lack of destination is debilitating. His anger is starting to shift down, way down. On autopilot, he's navigating through the streets without a compass. He never searched for an unknown-thought before, until now, until Pru came into his life. Then, out of the corner of his eye, he sees a fishtailing pick-up barreling toward him. Carney whips the steering wheel to the right and spins out of control through a wide-open intersection, coming to a stop on a gravel parking lot. He throws it into park and quickly looks for the truck, but there's nothing there. It was in his head.

He releases his emotions on the steering wheel. Hitting it like a punching bag—avoiding the horn—calling out with pain and outrage until his anger becomes tears, and his tears become laughter. He cries and laughs, scolds himself for scolding himself until drained of every emotion as if he fell into a peaceful meditative state. Then he naturally comes out of it, puts the car into gear, drives off, safely back onto a familiar road, and decides to follow through with Millennial's phone call.

"Hey Siri," he activates her responsive ears with a calmer voice. "Call Millennial."

He hears the ringing over his phone's speaker as he finally finds the freeway, only now he has to navigate through these unknown streets to find the onramp.

"Hey, man," Millennial says. "Thanks for getting back to me."

"Yeah, you know how things go. So what's up?"

"I got the IP to... well, maybe you know the book. It's that futuristic sci-fi Amazon Bestseller about a deaf man trying to find a utopian society called *Alfred's Pilgrimage.*"

Carney doesn't recall. Although it's not his usual genre, so he doesn't imagine he would.

"Well," Millennial continues, "I pitched it to Scott Manford, and he wants to see some pages. His production company is totally down to produce, and he'll tour it around to some studios for a collaboration. I mentioned that I'd like you to write, possibly direct, and he was super thrilled. I didn't know you two were friends when you were kids."

"He told you that?"

"Yeah, I think he said something about being in a movie with your dad. Was it *Two Donkeys and a Mule*?"

Carney tries to recall his preteen years, knowing it's either *Handel House* or *Two Donkeys and a Mule.* They were both filmed, back to back springs, in the prairie country. He remembers Scott wore a silly hat, high in the center but folded over like a regular cowboy hat, but it was called a mule. Now he recalls, it was *Two Donkeys and a Mule.*

"Yeah, it was," Carney replies, not sure if he's thankful for the trip back to his past.

Millennial moves on, "Right, well, what do you think? You want to come in on it with us?"

As Carney's forced to slow to a stop at a school crossing, his thoughts are a flashing caution yellow too until he catches eyes with a young boy that reminds him of himself, a kid more intense than he should be at that age, soaking up the life and pain around him. Carney is so far from his young self right now, when his eyes were sponges, eager for everything, and took any opportunity that came his way. So, seeing this kid before him as a sign, he agrees.

CHAPTER FIFTEEN

After reading *Alfred's Pilgrimage,* Carney spent his next two weeks, including Thanksgiving, attached to his laptop up in his loft, writing those pages for Millennial. All the while, promises of a meeting with Scott Manford are on the horizon. And Carney was readying his pitch, determined to direct as well.

Although he never lost sight of his girl during this time. He was attentive and drove Pru to all her appointments. Still, for the most part, she was easygoing and always available to listen to him when he needed to air out some thoughts and didn't mind forgoing Thanksgiving or a so-called Friends-giving dinner. She did not need for a big huff and fuss about a holiday. Not only had she lost the spirit long ago, but it allowed her the opportunity to get out of having to answer questions. Because she was sure that family would most certainly come up, besides that, she ran out of pain pills and had a hell-of-a-week. She tried cleaning up around the house to take her mind off of it, but she made too much noise for Carney. So she started reading a book. When she got to page eighty of *The Alchemist,* she was rewarded with a hundred dollar bill, stuck in between the pages like lost treasure to be bestowed to the discoverer. And sometimes Carney would go to Hemingway's to work, which worked out for her. She made friends with Mona, the tent dweller with braids directly across the boardwalk from Carney's beach house. Pru would bring her leftovers, and Mona would sell her oxycodone for twenty bucks a pop.

Then Pru began scouring the bookshelves for more treasure. She rationalized that it was unfair of the doctor to just cut her off. She had to taper down and get off gradually. Physical therapy was painful, but it was the quiet times that pained her most when she was left to her thoughts. Regret would try and creep in, like water during a flood oozing through her traumatic past, but she'd take a pill, and the floodwater would subside.

There's no need to medicate with Carney though, she enjoys her time with him more than anything, especially at night. Their world outside has been getting colder and darker, and their nest inside is bright and warm and filled with feathered pillows. The evenings are their time together, and they keep it simple, like a couple after dating a couple of months: movie on the couch and ordering in, only instead of what they are both wanting, because of her injured leg, it's followed by phone sex instead.

Tonight they plan to see Mae West in *I'm No Angel* after a game of gin rummy, which they haven't played since that first week back from the hospital, so Pru shuffles cards at the kitchen table with her leg up on a pillow.

"Yeah, hi," she says, over the phone embodying a Mae West accent. "We'll have your most popular dish. Don't tell me what it is. Just surprise us." Carney laughs, leaning against the counter after finishing the dishes, watching her, because everything she does fascinates him. "How will we pay?" She looks to him, never knowing how they'll pay.

"Cash," he calls back with an old-timey accent.

"Cash," she tells the order taker on the other end before listening. "Okay, that's fast. We'll see you then." She hangs up.

"You know, I have an app for that," he teases.

"Call me old-fashioned," she spats out one last Mae West for his pleasure. But there's nothing old-fashioned about her, other than that she lets him pay for everything.

He wonders what a dangerous woman like her looks like in domesticity. He imagines how many types she could pull off in the kitchen, but the sexy-dangerous circus performer wins out in the end, flinging knives into cork boards after washing them. Making a mental note for his untitled screenplay that he's finally able to get back to, he feels creative and wants to know all there is to know about her, every character flaw, strength, and original thought as if he thought it himself.

"I want you to tell me about the second guy," he says adamantly.

All her vitality fades from her face. She shuffles the cards more forcefully, avoiding or evading an answer.

He's not relenting, adding, "Something in your past you don't want me to know?"

To her, whenever she spoke of past relationships with a boyfriend, it never ended smoothly. She knows all too well that curiosity turns to jealousy faster than a fleeting bullet. She can sense Carney's destructive personality igniting, and she's not sure she can do anything about it.

"You know," she assesses, "it is possible to reconnect your neural pathways. You don't have to always press the self-sabotage button."

"You're dodging," he says, dismissing her assessment.

So she tries to reason with him, "You know, it's not normal to talk about exes."

"We're not normal," he reminds her.

"No, we're not," she agrees and laughs.

He is nowhere near like any of her exes. There was a bad boy quality she always went for, but it always seemed to bite her in the end because it wasn't strength or confidence that they possessed; it was false bravado. Something that doesn't exist in Carney. She wonders if she should listen to her advice, reconnect her neural pathways to tear down her walls. So she gives in.

"Just remember the past is the past," she urges.

"Sure."

He excitedly takes a seat across from her like he's got a front-row ticket to a one-person show and takes a swig from his frosty beer. She gears herself up to tell this, but she'll only be telling him the one time, once is all that's needed, for her sanity, at least.

"I was cocktailing at a bar in Long Beach when I met him," she says. Hoping he doesn't ask about what or who got her from Las Vegas to Long Beach. "He was night and day compared to Vegas. He did yoga, read books, and lived off the grid on his boat. We fell fast," she recalls sweetly before noticing a twinge of uneasiness on Carney's face. So she jumps ahead, "And one day he asked, so I quit my job and sailed with him to Hawaii. I learned more than I ever wanted to know about sailing and fishing and how to heal a sunburn while in the sun. It felt like we were lost at sea, but it was never that dire." She remembers the long days of blue sky and blue water, the endless rolling of swells that made her sick, and the repetition of it every day that brought out a fiery side in her. The irritation within her grew to an unbearable state that might have imploded to their own detriment had they not arrived on the island the following day. So she glosses over all of that baggage to get to the good stuff. "And Hawaii was great. We felt like the world was ours, and it was romantic, exciting." He listens, cringing a little inside. "I got a job selling catamaran tours in Waikiki, and he did hull cleaning and boat maintenance. We met interesting people, explored the other islands, and got into a really good routine. It was simple, and that was nice," she says, and it was nice for her. "But then *he* wanted to sail to Tahiti," she says grudgingly. Remembering the long arguments they had where he threatened her off the boat if she didn't want to go, and her rushing back to his side in full agreement. "And right before we were set to leave," she rushes through this part, "he had a heart attack underwater, and no one was there to save him, so he drowned."

If this is true, he knows he'll never be able to hold Pru's excitement. How can he compete with a sea-adventure? He's more convinced than ever that she'll recover and flee, and the best he can do is pull her story from her before she goes.

"What was he doing underwater?" he asks, in disbelief.

"Cleaning the hull of a boat, or stealing parts, who knows? He was that kind of guy."

That kind of guy?! he puzzles over.

"What did you do?" he presses her even more, like a director trying to ignite the character within.

Her voice takes a higher pitch, defensive tone, "What did I do, when? What could I do? I wasn't there." He waits for the one-woman show to continue, and with a less defensive tone, she drums on, "I helped pack up his things with his sister, and then I was on my own again."

He sees the frustration in her eyes. He knows for sure now that this is true, and the excitement in his eyes elevates.

"I was in a dark place," she continues, "spent a lot of time at the bar drowning my sorrows instead of myself. That's when..." She stops suddenly.

He looks around, wondering why the show stopped, and then realizes what it is: she suddenly realized what she was saying while she was saying it. Maybe it's something she's ashamed of, he thinks.

"When what?!" he probes on, "Is this when you met the next guy? The third one?"

She justifies, "You have to understand, we were two strangers grasping at life by grasping onto each other. Doomed from the start, but too blinded by the pain to see."

He's astonished. "Hold on, I gotta write that down." He fetches his laptop from his bag, like one of his excited students, and begins typing furiously in front of her, not realizing what he's doing. "You were grasping at life by grasping onto each other. Doomed, but blinded by...?" He gestures for her to recite it again.

"By the pain," she says, doing her best to be a good sport and not take offense, even though there's an undercurrent of a tone brewing in her throat.

"How long after him was it?" he probes, losing perspective.

"I'm sure you can imagine," she snaps with vigor.

And he can. He starts to break Pru down like a character. "How can you restart your heart so quickly? Either you're living off these guys, or you're one of those girls who falls in love too fast."

She dares to know what he means by that and replies, "One of those girls?"

He looks at her blankly, unaware of how he sounds. "Yeah, one of those girls. You're all looking for security. It's not love. It's comfort."

Her breath speeds up. "Yeah, I'm pretty comfortable right now. Shelter, food, and anything I could want. Good thing I don't want for much because I have a fucking awesome caretaker who's racked with guilt. I could probably get him to buy me anything I want." She looks at him with threatening eyes. She realizes she's his muse, but he's crossing the line. "So now I'm a character in your story?" she spats back rhetorically. "I mean, tell me when we're having a serious conversation," she demands with a sarcastic smile.

Becoming aware of what he's doing, he stares at her like she just exposed a nerve, and she stares back like the cat who caught the cockatoo.

Suddenly, there's a loud *KNOCK, KNOCK!* They both flinch like it's gunshots.

Then, understanding it must be their food, Carney gets up and goes to the door, taking out his wallet while she flips his laptop around to see what he's writing and reads, "Notes for Untitled Pru Story." Then she flips it back around before he returns. She had a feeling she was inspiring this Penny character, and she has to admit there's something complimentary about it. Who could possibly be offended? Although, she supposes he could get her all wrong and never get to understand her at all.

He sets the bag on the table, and through uncomfortable silence, he takes the squeaky styrofoam container from the crinkly plastic bag. Every sound echoes in their head where a conversation should be. He's too inspired to be sorry, and she's too amiable to be mad, but neither breaks the silence. He opens the container for the big reveal, and it's rotisserie chicken and fries.

"I'm sensing a theme," he says.

She laughs, breaking the tension, and he laughs with her. Their laughter develops to where they don't know what they're laughing at, laughing at each other, laughing that it's funny, or laughing because they both need to laugh. Tension is released. He gets two plates.

"You want to talk seriously?" His eyes intense as he divulges with an effort to be fair, "When I was a kid, I had kidnap training."

"Kidnap training?" she asks to see if she heard that right because she's never heard of such a thing.

He makes her a plate first, even though he's starving—that's what he does.

"My father had some nutty fans," he explains. "After death threats were sent to our home and the studio, he bumped up our security, and I got kidnap training, in case I was taken for ransom."

"Like what? What did they do?" she dives into his trauma head first with an effort to bond.

He breaks a leg off for a bite before continuing, "It's pretty simple how they broke it down to me as a kid.

Looking back, it was like a children's horror story." He dons a fairytale teller's voice and adds, "There's a little boy named Timmy and Timmy needs to know there are bad people out in the world who want to get him. Timmy probably won't be able to see them at first because the bad people like to hide. They might just swoop him up from behind and take him into a car or van."

She continues to nibble on her dinner with wide, captivated eyes, imagining young Carney in this scenario.

"I ran from white vans," he continues with his regular voice, "they terrified me." Biting into more of his chicken, he could eat a horse, and she can't take her eyes off him. She's riveted. He continues, "They taught me to scream 'help!' Imagine method acting for a seven-year-old, screaming with fear and anger over and over again. Screaming as if your life depended on it."

She looks horrified for him.

He continues with his fairytale voice, "Then Timmy needs to look, listen, and memorize." Back to a real voice, he says, "It was like playing that memory match game but in real life with real consequences. Terrifying when I couldn't remember my kidnappers' faces. It was like I failed my family. So I got better at studying people, seeing and hearing their moods, so I knew how to behave around them. The last thing they wanted me to do was piss off a kidnapper with a killer instinct while I waited to be rescued. So I got to know them in my imagination. We became friends, actually."

For the first time, she sees more to him than she previously thought. She knew he's soft around the edges compared to her and a little too enchanted by her dark side, but now she sees he has his own dark corners.

"Sounds like you know a little about singing for your supper, too," she chirps back.

He nods, enjoying his bird with his story dismissed back to the past, and she enjoys her new view of him. He's become more than a good-on-paper guy, more than a stable kind caretaker; he can relate, and to her, there is no better turn-on than someone who understands pain. Hope is again on the horizon, and instantaneously she wonders, what will go wrong?

CHAPTER SIXTEEN

The Home Depot is scarce of customers but stacked to the gills with holiday lighting, faux trees, and decorations as Carney wheels Pru down the front of the store, whistling the ominous theme song to his dad's western, *Two Donkeys And A Mule.* He finally got word from Millennial that his meeting with Scott Manford is set for Christmas Eve, an early dinner.

He would usually take a holiday meeting as a good omen, but he's never been a fan of the holidays. It only reminds him of his childhood home, decorated to the gills with Christmas cheer and as quiet as a ghost town while his parents made the rounds of parties and events, and he experienced the vast rotation of sitters who didn't want to be there.

"Which aisle?" he asks, realizing he's pushing her aimlessly around for an idea that could only be hers.

"It'll be on one of the ends," she says knowingly.

"How do you know that? You date a guy from Home Depot?"

"Not everything I know comes from a man," she quips.

"But you dated a lot of guys, right?" he insinuates, his tone, borderline condemnatory.

"How is it that you write women?" she fires back playfully.

He laughs. "Obviously, not ones like you."

"Well, let me give you a tip," she begins, with an effort to help him understand his Penny a bit more, "women can be familiar with Home Depot and fall in love fast. It's easy to see flaws and build walls. It's harder to see the good outweighs the bad and decide to love anyway." And without missing a beat, she points, "There it is! Wood."

He turns the wheelchair to go down the wood aisle. She immediately scans each stack, reading its corresponding tag. "Sycamore, birch, oak." She knows they're in the hardwood section, so she keeps looking, and he keeps pushing.

"I still think this is medieval," he contests.

"Oh, come on," she teases, "you'll be begging to tie me to a board soon enough."

His eyes quickly dart for people, worried that their privacy could be invaded. A knee-jerk reaction being a McMorris, anyone in earshot could be a future problem. One time, his father mentioned to a friend over lunch that he was taking young Carney and his wife, Gloria, Carney's mom, on a vacation in Puerto Vallarta. Someone must have overheard at the restaurant because the next thing they knew, they were bombarded with so much paparazzi that they couldn't even leave their bungalow. It's not that Carney thinks his private life is of anyone's interest or that he's anything like his father. It's just a habit he'll never shake. He'll always be looking to censor himself for the good of a man that died a decade ago.

There's no one in their aisle or nearby, but he whispers anyway. "Maybe sooner than later." Imagining her in a sexy black lace something-or-other strapped to his bed.

She smiles playfully back to remind him that she's more than interested because she has fantasized about being in bed with him too, and the almost nightly phone sex is doing more for him than for her. All it does is build upon her already existing desire so that when he kisses her, she doesn't want it to stop, but her damn leg is holding them back. For her, that's even more reason to get this.

"Grab that one," she says, seeing the one-by-fours made of poplar.

He grabs it. "It's too long."

"We cut them to size," she informs him as if she's an employee.

His frustration level is reaching red. He's doing a good job concealing it, but he's about ready to turn around and veto the idea altogether. "I could've just bought you the damn contraption for all this work," he reasons.

"Waste of money," she proclaims, recalling the doctor informing them it's only nine-hundred dollars as if everyone has an extra nine-hundred laying around. She'll probably only use it a few days at the most. So there's no way she can justify that kind of frivolous expenditure, even if it is his money. "This is all we need to get me straight," she insists, measuring her leg with her arm because she strangely knows her forearm—wrist to elbow—is ten inches. "Tell the guy we need four feet."

He doubts her leg will straighten this way, but he looks around for the guy even though this makes him feel helpless and out of place. Not knowing where to look for a Paul Bunion in an orange apron, he stands there immobile with an eight-foot board.

She gauges his lack of familiarity and guesses, "I'd bet you had carpenters and gardeners and..."

"Maids," he finishes her sentence. "That reminds me, she should be finishing about now. Thank God, because I'm way overdue. She used to come every other week," he says before he spots an older man in an orange apron.

Pru starts to panic. All she can think about is the maid and the gun that's under the mattress. She's all but caught.

In the car, she asks, "How can you trust anyone in your house when you're not there?"

"Good thing I do," he says, referring to her.

She smiles awkwardly, knowing he wouldn't be too pleased to find out she took his gun and the hidden treasure from his bookshelf. Then used the money to buy black market pain pills from their homeless neighbor.

"Maybe you shouldn't," she remarks. "You're too trusting."

That doesn't make him feel at ease, and it doesn't seem like the words of someone who's singing for their supper. He thinks it sounds like someone who's giving advice because they have one foot out the door. But all she's thinking about is the gun. Will the maid think it's hers? Or does the maid know it belongs to Carney? Will she tell Carney about it or keep it where it is? What kind of relationship does he have with his maid? She can only assume that the maid worked for his father, which would make her like family, which she sums up that the maid would definitely tell him about the gun, either way. So she needs to prepare a defense argument, but as she tries to bottle up an explanation, she realizes that the trust will be broken either way. He'll know she's a thief, and then that's all she'll ever be.

Her heart races the entire way home, and as soon as she enters his place, she beelines her walker over to her freshly made bed. Sitting in her regular position, she slides her hand under the mattress. There it is. Her hand slides over the grip, and her finger glides over the trigger. It hasn't moved. She knows because if the maid found it and put it back under the mattress, there's no way it would be in the exact same place. She lets her fingers feel some more and finds both the pills, wrapped in foil, and the folded up money. She sighs in relief just as Carney comes out from his room, reluctantly holding up two worn leather belts.

"Will this work?"

She's quick to be natural. "Give it here, Romeo."

It saddens him she wants to speed up her recovery because it's not often that he wants a woman to stick around past her expiration date. He's partially bitter on the whole idea of love and marriage since his parents couldn't make it work, but Pru makes him reconsider. Having this sense that she wants to leave him is definitely not the turn he wanted for the day.

He gets the four-foot board from the hallway and comes to her sluggishly, handing her the belts before the board of wood. She overlooks his mood shift; it's easy for her not to notice, in her mind, she's just escaped the firing range. Lifting her left hip, she slides the board underneath and straps one belt above her knee and one belt below. Slowly she begins to tighten, one at a time, until the pain is almost unbearable. Breathing through it, she feels under her knee to see how much it's flattened: two fingers to go. Her therapist said it's possible to walk with a bent leg, but she's determined not to walk like a pirate. Holding the pain until she can't anymore, she releases the belts to let her leg bend naturally back to its comfortable position, and he looks at her with agony on his face.

She starts again, tighter this time, which isn't much more. Her knee moves closer to the board, and she's really feeling the pain now. Sensing with her fingers to see how far away she is, she's just over a finger width. Tightening it some more, it barely moves. She holds it there, taking slow, long breaths.

He watches with consternation.

She knows how much pain she can handle life has shown her it's an enormous amount and thinks his concern for her is sweet, but that's not what's going on with him. Only he doesn't know what's going on. His eyes suddenly sadden in seconds, it's uncontrollable, and she sees it on his face right away.

"What's wrong?" she asks, loosening the straps.

He's never had this happen to him before. Feeling embarrassed, he turns around to hide his emotions.

"Are you okay?" she worries, getting to her walker.

His eyes water like there's a leak in his dive suit, and any second, it will bust over the side and form tears, and there's nothing he can do to stop it. He wonders if it's an allergic reaction. Then it comes, tears one and two fall and drip on his shirt. Thinking for a moment that he's experiencing some brain trauma from the accident, but he had a full-body test and an exam and came out fine. Suddenly, he feels the urge to cry out, a grief-stricken moan that sounds like an animal dying.

"I don't know what the fuck is going on with me," he lets out with hostility before disappearing into his bedroom.

He paces for a moment before sitting on the edge of his bed, putting his head in his hands and releases a burst of sniveling tears. Then downshifts it to a breathy metronome, like he's hyperventilating.

She enters with her walker.

He waves his hand at her and says, "No. Get out, please."

"No," she insists, "you're going to talk to me."

"Fuck! I don't want to talk!" he yells, letting her know he is serious. "Get the fuck out of my room!"

But she doesn't back down; she mirrors his energy. "You want to see anger?" She grips her walker so ferociously that if she had superpowers, she would have ripped through the handles like butter and holds it out like a weapon.

"I'll throw this across the fucking room!" she threatens with a screeching tone. "Let's go crazy!"

He acknowledges she went from zero-to-crazy in one second, and she's not even acting. He can see it in her eyes. She will do it and most likely hurt herself in the process. Adrenaline is rushing through his body rapidly because he knows there is no limit to what a woman in rage could do. Their normal logic vanishes as their body is taken over by hormones—they are like a zombie. He gains control of himself with the singular aim to calm her down immediately.

"Whoa, whoa, whoa," he says, holding out his arms as if she is aiming a gun.

She barters, "Are you going to talk to me?"

"Okay, okay!" he capitulates.

She quickly calms her demeanor like a sprinting cheetah slamming on the brakes and walks to him with her walker, sitting beside him on the bed as if nothing happened.

He's exhausted and amazed by how she controlled his emotions, and he's even more uncertain now if she's a good bet or his own worst nightmare. But that doesn't matter because she has him by the balls, his balls and his brain, his creative impulses and his fantasy for danger, toppled with the most erotic package he's ever wanted to unwrap.

Forcing an answer to the surface to explain what has him so emotional, he says, "It's hard to see you in pain after everything you've been through."

"Bullshit!" she calls him out, asking him to look deeper. "What's really going on?"

"I honestly don't know," he says with complete sincerity. "It's like that feeling in a movie when everything is going good, and then music plays, so you know something bad is going to happen. That music is playing."

She listens with understanding.

He continues to try and describe it. "It's like a flood, like a..." He motions with tense hands to his chest.

"You're falling in love with me," she says with temerity.

He busts with laughter. "That's funny!"

"I know what a guy looks like when he's falling in love."

"Of course, you would!" he quips, still laughing.

She realizes that she should have chosen better words, but she won't let that distract her from what's really going on.

She declares, "I'm not an earthquake, you know. You don't have to be afraid."

"I'm not afraid of earthquakes. I just want to be prepared."

"You can never be prepared for love," she says. Thinking, *he should know that...* Then realizes, asking, "You've never been in love?"

"I've been in love," he insists.

"You can't bluff around me anymore. I know all your faces. I study you every time we talk, and even when we don't." She looks at him in a spidery way that would turn off most men, but only turns him on. "Don't you study me?" she asks rhetorically, knowing he does.

The silence hangs in the air as he realizes they're probably both watching the other sleep and thinks maybe she doesn't have one foot out the door. They could even be a better match than he's been betting on; being the object-of-her-affection is far better than what he's used to, being the son of their object-of-affection, the main reason most of his relationships are doomed. Because to him, love has always seemed borrowed and owed and then borrowed and owed again like some fictional story thread always ending in catastrophe. But Pru's affection seems natural, a calming wind, and the fact that she hasn't told him excites him like it's a game. He's never connected with another person like this before. He kisses her passionately, and she runs her hand through his hair. Her kiss tells him she wants more, so he docks his boat on her shore and discovers the mountainous land under her shirt. Her skin is soft and warm, and her aureoles tighten into knots. Then it suddenly occurs to him that she doesn't have her leg lifted. He knows her circulation is still not back to normal, and after working her leg on that board, she's in for some swelling, so he stops kissing her and offers her some ice.

She wonders if they could've kept going, but she's always been slow to make decisions because she often feels incapable of discriminating between what's good and bad for her. It's part of the reason why she orders food the way she does. She puts it in someone else hands. In the way that ancient societies put their faith in the gods, blindly.

CHAPTER SEVENTEEN

Pru wonders if this year, she will have a traditional Christmas Eve dinner. Although traditional to her is like a foreign word, her parents' idea of Christmas Eve was to invite over friends and visiting travelers for a potluck. There were no traditional food or traditions of any kind. Not like when she's been a visitor to someone else's house for the holiday. Those occasions felt cozy and comforting. Wishing she could order that, but instead, she puts it in the hands of the young waiter who answers the phone. She always assumes and never expects so that she's not left disappointed. She assumes she'll receive a holiday dinner, but didn't check to see if they were doing anything special, so she holds no expectations. All she tells him is that it would be for two, in case Carney wants leftovers when he comes home from his meeting, and if he doesn't, then it'll be a wonderful treat for her homeless neighbor outside.

In a private booth in the back corner of Mastro's Steak House, Carney is waiting for Scott Manford to arrive. Scott's late by fifteen minutes, but what did he expect? Actors of Scott Manford's realm set their watches to their own time, but Carney had higher expectations for Scott. They go way back to when they were kid actors auditioning for similar parts. He knew Scott was going to succeed in this business. They had a similar work ethic, only Scott never had the skin problems Carney had. Luckily, the restaurant is mostly empty, so no one will see Carney dabbing his forehead, the sweaty mess he is. He tells himself it's all the holiday decorations raising his blood pressure, so he doesn't acknowledge the disrespect he feels boiling up inside. Scott is an actor, and actors show up late to meetings these days. Even though he recalls how punctual his father was and how insistent his father was that he always be on time.

Pru, meanwhile, gets up to answer the door. It's times like these, when she is alone, that she wishes Carney's front door had a peephole, so she looks through the kitchen window, and as expected, it's her holiday dinner delivery.

She opens the door and manages the walker and the passing over of money for food quite well. The hard part is taking it back to the table. It's too big for her walker bag, so she holds it by the handles of its plastic bag and lets it swing back and forth under the walker with each hobbled step. Sinatra's "White Christmas" is playing on the KOST 103.5 radio station, which she's taking full opportunity to play loudly while Carney's away. She opens her containers, assuming it will be either ham or turkey with sides of stuffing and mashed potatoes, but it's tacos! Tacos filled with pumpkin, black beans, and guacamole. She doubts her meat-eating man will enjoy this, so she puts the containers back in the bag and hobbles out to the patio.

"Mona," she calls out toward the blue tent.

Mona peeks out, and when she sees the bag that Pru holds up, her face illuminates. "Hell-oo."

"Merry Christmas, happy holidays, or whatever the fuck," Pru laughs off.

"Same to you, sister," Mona says, climbing up on the stucco patio wall, taking one of the containers from Pru with a smile. "Thank ye, thank ye."

Pru sits on the sofa chair and digs into a pumpkin taco with the holiday flare she's accustomed to.

"Is that 'Jingle Bells' I hear?" Mona checks in to see if Pru's skepticism is still intact.

Pru listens, hearing what is undoubtedly "Jingle Bells."

"What can I say?" Pru chimes. "I'm feeling the holiday cheer this year."

Mona laughs at how silly that is, and Pru joins in. It's reckless to have this much hope, and she knows it.

Pru asks bluntly, "So how did you become homeless?"

Mona finishes chewing one of the tacos and laughs, a depressing, bitter laugh. "I ran out of friends with floors, after running out of friends with couches, after losing my job, after losing my mom."

Mona takes a bite of the next taco, while Pru swallows the hard truth that it's a fine line between her and the streets, made even more complicated by her injury.

"But I won't be homeless for long," Mona insists. "I'm really a Kardashian, and as soon as I get my ass back, I can prove it. I told my lawyer I wouldn't tell anyone, so don't say anything."

Pru can see now that Mona isn't playing with a full deck. She's away with the fairies, so to speak, and incapable of a day job until properly medicated. She should be in a mental institution to get her equilibrium worked out.

Pru figures *we're all capable of busting a chip in the ol' hardware at some point* and doesn't hold any judgment.

"You in love with the loud talker?" Mona points to Carney's house.

Loud talker? Pru laughs inside her head. Born Italian, she's practically immune to loud talkers.

As for loving him, she's incapable of knowing. She thinks he could be in love, but that's just a hunch. He hasn't said it yet, so she shouldn't let down her guard. Any moment she could be on her ass, like Mona, hoping someone shares a meal with her. Pru's world is as fragile as a candle in a cold breeze, and a breeze cometh. She grabs the colorful Mexican blanket from the back of the sofa chair and wonders if the cold wind is a harbinger for trouble ahead. She thinks of Carney and hopes his meeting is going well. He deserves some good news.

Knee deep into his second glass of beer, Carney relaxes back into the booth, smiling, while Scott Manford wraps up a highly entertaining anecdote that he started after their typical, "Good to see you, man. How the hell have you been?" introductory foreplay, followed by, "Let's order." Scott's a professional. He knows how to entertain. Whether he wants something from this meeting or not, he knows the value of leaving a good impression because an actor is only as good as his ability to be cast.

Carney's enjoying himself. Not only is it good to catch up with his old friend, but it takes him back to the only time in his life when he really felt free and alive.

Before the steaks arrive, he asks, "So Scott, what about this story got your interest?"

Scott wrinkles his brows. "I don't know anything about it. I was told you wanted to throw a pitch by me."

A hefty blow to Carney. *Gasp!* He realizes he's just been bamboozled by a friend in his inner circle.

Scott can see it on Carney's face, so he changes the subject. "Do you remember that time we met? I had to be nine or ten, and your father was amazing. I really felt like he was my father, not just playing one for the cameras. Not a holiday passes by where I don't think of him, but you know how that is."

Carney nods. "So, you don't know who set this up?"

"My agent," Scott recalls. "He said you wanted to meet."

Carney drinks his beer down, his synapses firing insults at himself, acknowledging that he spent the last two weeks or more working on those pages for Millennial without a contract or payment because of friendship. He remembers what Pru said about him being too trusting and thinking she's right. He now knows Millennial is a liar, and it would do him no favors to speak of it any further to Scott. It would only expose Carney's own misfortune for having chosen such a deceitful friend.

Taking the conversation back into a personal direction, Carney says, "We had some good times growing up in this town."

"Good times, for sure," Scott reminisces. "You know, I so wanted that part in *Skateboard Heaven*, and when I heard you got it, I wasn't so upset anymore. And when it came out, and I saw it, I was like, man, no one could have captured Grinder as you did. You were amazing, man. You were him. You will always be Grinder to me."

Compliments of a time long gone wash over Carney's head like a cold shower, but he holds it in and lets Scott enjoy his trip. Memory lane is only good for the one who's driving the car, and Carney feels like the hitchhiker that's been picked up half a block back.

CHAPTER EIGHTEEN

Carney smokes a cigar outside the building where Pru receives her physical therapy. The chilly wind whips the smoke into a ghostly swirl as he watches Pru through the glass with intensely focused eyes.

She is doing the same exercise as she did the day before, standing face to face with her handsome therapist. The two rods in his hands are the only thing holding her balance. She laughs because it reminds her of how she danced in middle-school. But all Carney sees is how close they are, too close for his comfort, and her laughter is so animated she is almost bending over with hysteria. He wonders, *do I make her laugh like that?* Slowly she steps forward, and the therapist steps back, both in sync, their eyes committed to one another, perhaps too committed from Carney's perspective. He watches, his eyes like a 200-millimeter lens so magnified he overanalyzes her every expression, forming a story in his head—that's what he does. Is she planning on leaving him after she is healed and setting up this guy to be next? All he can see is the elation on her face. Her smile is wider than any she has given him. Then she throws her arms around her therapist like she's not even trying to hide it. And he hugs her back! *Doesn't she know I'm watching?* Suddenly, she turns her eyes to look right at Carney, so he turns around, acting like he didn't see them. He doesn't want her to see that his face is wracked with obsession.

Just then, a white van drives by, alerting his senses from kidnap training. The unmarked van is larger than a minivan but smaller than a truck, with no government plates. So it is civilian, he deducts, and definitely suspicious. He watches it, hoping there are no kids around. And then, as it pulls up to park outside a nearby coffee house, he sees there is a kid! He's sitting outside with a young woman as a man gets out of the van in a black hoodie and baseball hat and goes to open the sliding side door. Carney notices his heart racing. He wonders, *has it been racing this whole time?* And getting ready to make a mad dash to rescue the boy, but he pauses and watches as the door opens. The guy looks at the kid, but the guy is not alone. Out of the van comes a cameraman and a gaffer.

Carney takes a puff from his cigar to calm his nerves and watches them set-up for a gorilla film production. He should feel relief that it's not a kidnapping, but his nerves can't quite settle. Wondering if it's lingering effects of Millennial's blatant betrayal, or maybe it's something more than that. A twinge irks him seeing the hopeful faces of these young filmmakers, remembering feeling that way, before the roadblocks and dead ends, he was committed to making it as a director/writer without relying on his dad or his dad's friends. Torturing himself now for how it's turned out, the mistakes he would do over, and people he wouldn't have invested in, and suddenly there's a loud tapping on the glass.

He turns to see Pru with her walker pushed hard against the window with wide eyes.

"I'm walking!"

Carney immediately realizes why she was so joyous with her therapist. She was happy to be walking, and she celebrated with that guy instead of him, even though he was right there. He could've easily seen her walking if he wasn't so caught up with his own dramatic unraveling.

He forces a smile. "That's great."

"See, I don't give up," she calls out through the glass and motions for him. "Watch this."

Smoking, he watches her practice walking, a few steps at a time, then falls into the arms of her therapist again. Carney forces another smile, wanting to be happy for her, but he also knows that her walking changes everything. Now she doesn't need him anymore. The big question for him is, will she fly away from their nest? As she sets herself up again, he watches every step with the guilt of missing the first one.

He beats himself up for not being there for her. *What am I doing? Am I going to let a shadow of doubt tear down every wall in my house?* And he vows to be better. He has always hated fear because fear will get you nowhere, and nothing becomes from fear—fear gets you dead.

After extinguishing his cigar into the landscape rocks, he walks up the ramp toward the entrance with the vigor of a man who is determined to get what he wants. And right now, he wants her to walk into his arms.

CHAPTER NINETEEN

Mitch McMorris looks fierce in a long black trench coat and eyes like steel. The Colt Army Revolver hangs heavy in his right hand, and his other drags a dying, bleeding man by his collar over to Hops and his running truck, dropping him down right there. Then turns and walks away.

"You're going to walk? Alone?" Hops asks. "Don't you want the money?"

"We all walk alone, man," Mitch declares, without looking back.

The music rises, in the sound of a steel guitar, and he keeps walking. Filling the entire tv frame—his expression deeply satisfied. Pru watches from the couch as the credits roll over Mitch's face—her expression deeply satisfied.

She turns her head toward the empty space on the couch next to her and wishes Carney were there. He's on the back patio, talking loudly on the phone, for Mona and the collective of beach bums and tourists to hear, and Pru laughs to herself.

Carney doesn't mind the loud traffic before him on this exceptionally-warm winter day. It will only drown out the pain in his voice, pain that sounds like anger.

His eyes are focused like his father's in the final scene of *Walking Alone*. Except he's not fighting bad guys in a movie. He's fighting against the injustice of friendship.

"You can't be trusted," Carney declares to Millennial, who has the lack of respect to further attempt to reel him in.

Carney could never fathom the overt lying and false boasting for a business deal, and he doesn't see how Millennial thinks he can get away with it. Even now, all Carney is getting are excuses and one falsely-felt apology that seems pulled off the internet. A distorted sense of depth that appears devoid of a human being. Yet even though he is the wronged one in this scenario, he is still making an effort to keep the essence of the friendship in existence because Carney doesn't partake in the he-said-he-said bullshit. He'd rather walk away unless he's fighting for his character, but this isn't that—this is among his inner cigar circle of friends, and he'd rather stay friends from afar before letting the whole group know about it. Eventually, time will cast its shadow on the villain without Carney having to lift a finger. No doubt, the friendship will never be the same, but Carney asks himself if it was really a friendship to begin with.

He remains outside even after getting off the phone, letting his disgust settle into the bottom of his beer glass. The uneasiness in his mind has him questioning other things he supposed were true. Are there other reasons why he keeps getting rejected for directing gigs? Has he been blackballed and doesn't know it? Is Millennial the only two-faced friend he has over there at Hemingway's, or are they all conspiring against him? False narratives are raging inside him, which leads him back to Pru. She blatantly told him that he shouldn't trust people in his house when he's not around, basically admitting she shouldn't be trusted. Which begs the question, what dishonest behavior could she be up to? What precisely about her shouldn't be trusted? What she says or what she does? She's been an angel of a house guest, really accommodating, clean, and quiet, but he's starting to wonder, is she singing for her supper? What does he really know about her, that she's possibly a serial dater with a vagabond mentality, on the run from reality?

He comes back inside, so she immediately looks up at him from her phone and tucks it out of sight, between her thigh and couch. He wonders what she's hiding. He can't help himself.

Joining her on the couch, he sees the end-credits roll on tv. "It's already over? I didn't know I was on the phone that long."

"That's okay," she assures him, putting her hand on his thigh. "It was cool watching it, knowing that's your dad."

"Where are your parents?" he asks, not knowing if she'll answer but determined to get an answer from her either way.

She looks out the window and pulls her hand back. "They left when I turned eighteen, fled to Italy after congratulating themselves on raising me to adulthood," she states with a sarcastically pleasant tone. "After a while, they just stopped calling, maybe so did I."

Finally, he's getting somewhere. He could guess it is abandonment issues, which would explain a lot. Carney has his own abandonment issues from his father being unavailable for long periods-of-time during his life. Although he still had his mother; until she left, not of her own causes, further deepening the wound. He suspects she longs for that missing time with her parents, the way he did with his dad.

"What were they like?" he asks, hoping to draw more out of her.

She takes a deep breath and begins to get up. "You hungry?"

"I'll get it," he offers, hoping her window of disclosure hasn't closed.

"No, I need to get better at walking," she insists. Taking the shiny new cane he bought for her, she cautiously walks toward the kitchen, focusing on each step.

Seeing her phone unlocked, he grabs it, wanting to know what she was looking at when he came through the door. He opens her text messages, but there are only ones from him. So he clicks on her recent calls, and it's all him and restaurants, or what he assumes are restaurants because there are no contacts listed. She has no contacts at all. Only him and "Physical Therapy."

"I'll bct you'll bc thrillcd whcn you can drivc again," he tests.

"Maybe your Nova," she teases, almost to the kitchen, "but let's not put the trolley before the horse."

She walks slow and controlled into the kitchen while he snoops into her photos. He sees pictures of her leg, x-rays, beach, birds, and him sleeping. Her last one taken was a moody black-and-white of him on the phone outside. Realizing she's not hiding anything other than a painful past, he puts her phone back on the couch where he found it.

"You never get a phrase right," he states, playfully, before she starts the walk back with popcorn.

"What are you talking about? What phrases?" she asks.

"Just now, trolley before the horse."

"What's it supposed to be?"

"Cart," he tells her. "Don't put the cart before the horse."

She laughs, sitting back on the couch a little out of breath.

"You do that on purpose, right?"

"No," she laughs, thinking he must be joking, and leans her body into his. "I love that you can make me laugh."

He looks at her enthralled like she just said I love you, even more of a reason to not let her off easy.

"So, what were they like, your parents?"

She knows she's cornered, and she can't evade him anymore. He's finally stopped being patient and started demanding answers. It's implied, the time is up. She'll have to fold her cards to stay in the game. In a way, she's kind of proud of him. He's really playing cards like a professional now.

She tells him about growing up in Santa Barbara and how she felt like an orphan in her own house. That she was bullied at school for being weird, but he suspects it was for being beautiful. Beautiful women are usually isolated from the herd. He learns that she had difficulty connecting with anyone unless they weren't human. She was friends with horses and dogs, insects, and birds, until her teenage years. Then boys became her orbit, her teachers, her friends. When her parents tried to take that away, she ran away.

He can't believe that she's opening up like this. He figures it can only be because she's finally letting her guard down to trust him. Ironic, since he was just starting not to trust her, he almost feels ashamed of that, but he wants to trust her completely. She's a sympathetic character, he thinks, and inspiration hits him. He spends the next three-weeks writing about how Penny and the fisherman, named James Finnegan, form a relationship while on his small fishing boat. Turns out he is a captain, after all, and she's got a few bucks to give for his time, so she commissions him to take her to Mexico. He's compassionate for her reasons, fleeing from a villainous man, but he tries to convince her he can protect her. He likes her company. Although, his first-mate, Long Beard, is forming his own conclusions for her sudden arrival and hurried departure. The old man with the long beard has a healthy distrust for transient women. He is convinced she's the Raven Bank Bandit he's been hearing about on his favorite weekly news broadcast. Long Beard's greed overtakes his friendship and loyalty to James as he plots a plan instead and hijacks the boat at gunpoint on their way to Mexico. A struggle ensues between Long Beard and James, and just before Long Beard pulls the trigger, Penny puts an end to it. *Bang! Bang!* Long Beard is dead. Only, while deciding whether to dispose of his body overboard or bury it once on land, a Mexican *Federales* boat announces themselves and commands to come on board.

While Carney and Pru drink champagne, waiting for the New Years' clock to tick down, he goes to the bookshelf to read her a quote from *The Alchemist*, and her eyes go wide. He flips through the pages to find the section and notices the hundred dollar bill he hid there is missing.

He flips through the pages some more like he can't find the quote, doing an exceptional impression of being none the wiser, that's the actor in him, and still cannot find the money. Then he locates the quote and reads it to her. They have a fully fleshed conversation about the validity of following your heart wherever it takes you. Agreeing on the issue. All the while, he imagines her taking the money from his book. Like she took the money at the casino. He wonders if this may be her flaw, maybe her one and only. She can't be trusted around money. But he thinks back to when he gave her money for takeout, and she returned him all the change. That's small change, he reasons, but what if it weren't? What if? What if? He could play this game all night. She's an enigma, and he can't deny that he's falling for her, so some faults might have to be acceptable; because he doesn't want to walk alone, without her.

CHAPTER TWENTY

Carney stands in front of his new semester of students taking roll call and studying faces. It is an oddball bunch of film novices with open notebooks and upright pens. The class is much fuller than his previous one, which makes him contemplate the reason why. Is he a better teacher now that Pru is in his life? He did receive high evaluation marks from his students last semester. It also may be that his name has started to circulate through word of mouth. It is just as easy for bad word of mouth to spread if his students felt the opposite way, his namesake goes both ways, and for the last several years, it hasn't moved either way. She has opened up something inside him he can measure simply by class size.

He dares to take it a step further. So he gathers up his students, herding them outside to sit out in the courtyard. They look awkward and uncomfortable sitting cross-legged on the cold grass, but he doesn't want them to feel comfortable. Comfort breeds ill performance, and they won't find that in the real world.

"The first thing you should know," Carney professes, "is that L.A. is a deck of cards stacked against you, even if you're born into it like me. The longer you survive in this Hollywood habitat, the more you will understand that nothing is fair. The cart sometimes comes before the horse, and the earth can open up at any time." His students accept his approach with wide eyes and open minds.

He stands in the center of them, closes his eyes, and holds his arms out wide like Andy Dufresne in the redemptive rain in *Shawshank Redemption.* "And there's nothing you can do. You can plan and prepare. You can think you're in control. Until something happens, and you're forced to improvise," he says, opening his eyes like he's had a spiritual awakening, "but that's when the movie magic happens. Either you adapt, or you lose the light." The class absorbs his words, and their pens begin to write into their notebooks.

Meanwhile, at home, Pru stacks up all of her belongings. It's difficult for her to manage because she can't carry anything while walking and can only use one hand because her other helps balance herself with a cane.

She packs her clothes into a bag and drags it, one step at a time, to a pile in the hallway until her area in the living room is all cleared out. After unmaking the bed and throwing the dirty sheets in the garage, she steps back to survey her landscape when it hits her. The gun! She lifts the edge of the mattress and pulls it out. For a moment, she considers putting it back in its case but then figures against it.

Carney rolls into the garage and parks next to his now repaired motorcycle. He's been planning to get back on the horse, but he's been putting it off. Maybe it's the tunnel vision he gets into when writing. Or perhaps he's nervous about how it would make him feel. Either way, he's putting it off.

He enters the pitch-black house and knows something is up. She always has the television on even if she falls asleep. He wonders if there was a power outage, so he hastily turns the light on in the kitchen, and it comes on, and the microwave says the correct time. In the living room, he looks at her bed, but she's not there, and her stuff is gone. She's gone!

His heart aches to see his living room back to how it was before she arrived, the mattress still in the middle of the room. It only stands now as a burning reminder that she once existed in his life. He starts to freak out. He has no idea where she could've gone, and the fact that she could vanish without warning scares the hell out of him. He can't look at his living room anymore. She will forever haunt his house like a ghost.

After shutting off the light, he grabs a beer from the fridge. Dwelling in the dark will be his new state of existence. That's when he sees it, a glowing firelight emanating from his bedroom. Fire! He rushes to get the extinguisher and collides with the wall, snaps it loose, and hightails into his bedroom, but there's no fire. Candles are everywhere, and Pru is spread out on the bed like a curvaceous wildcat in black lacy lingerie.

"What took you so long?" she asks.

He drops the fire extinguisher to the floor, laughing like a madman. "I thought you left and started a fire," he says, exhausted from his emotional roller coaster ride.

"You thought I started a fire?"

Still cautious of offending her, he wishes he could take it back. But to his surprise, she doesn't care.

"I thought we could start one together," she purrs, patting the bed for him to come like he's a dog. "It's about time we finish our second date."

"I'd like that," he says, overwhelmed by her power to cripple him.

He sits on the bed watchful of her leg, and she runs her hands through his thick pompadour. He doesn't bother with any questions. Logic isn't driving his car at the moment. For all he knows, this could be a farewell song, but anything past her lips is a blur. He kisses her with the fire that rages inside and simultaneously strips his clothes off.

"Oh, and," she says, stopping mid-momentum, "I moved my stuff into your room. I hope that's okay. I don't want to sleep in the living room anymore."

He sighs in relief.

He could warn her that he doesn't sleep much, and the light is always on. Or that he'll worry about her leg so high up on the bed. But all that doesn't seem to matter much right now. She's not going anywhere.

"It's more than okay," he says, kissing her, while every once in awhile admiring how sexy she is in the lingerie.

He doesn't see her scars. All he is focused on is how barely the black lace covers her breast and how easily it is to move aside. Being with her is better than how he imagined. He maneuvers in between her legs, and she arches her back when he kisses her neck. He handles her like he's borrowing a friend's Ferrari: delicately. His passion for her is revving up until he has to down-shift with caution for her leg. And like swerving around a hazard in the road, they are back on course. They've been wishing for this moment for so long, and finally, it's here. It's hot in this car, almost too hot to handle for both of them, but eventually, they find their speed. Nothing else matters but the two of them and this moment.

CHAPTER TWENTY ONE

Hand and hand, and cane, Carney and Pru walk down the boardwalk together, gazing out at the world like they're in a fishbowl. As if the world is a zoo only existing for their viewing, and they are just visitors. Strangely enough, Carney really does feel like a visitor. For he has an entirely different outlook on his life than he did when he ran into her that day, the day of the accident, that many months ago. He's no longer looking for fulfillment outside himself. Or for some project, or accolades hence after to feed his soul. He feels the skin of his past shed away, and for the first time in his life, he's living life instead of letting life live him.

The beachfront is mostly clear this afternoon, most likely due to the offshore winds irritating the common tourist, but the wind doesn't bother them. Nothing could break their bubble. It's a special occasion. Pru's out of the house for a reason other than physical therapy or doctor appointments. She couldn't be happier and even put on a pretty floral dress to commence the day, even though she has to hold it down from the cyclonic breeze that swirls around them ever so often. Nothing could break her mood. Hope and trust are penetrating her heart giving her newborn feelings of safety in his arms, and it has been way too long since she had that feeling with a man. She was as low as Carney suspected that day in Vegas when they met—not rob a bank low but almost desperate.

"I had this dream last night," she confesses. "A reoccurring dream that I've been having for years."

"Oh yeah?" he says, wanting to hear more.

"I'm falling down a cliff face, but the cliff disappears. So I'm in mid-air falling, and right before I hit the ground, I wake up."

He listens with the patience of a priest.

She continues, "It hits me from time to time, and it's always the same, until last night. Last night I dreamed that I'm falling down the cliff face again, but this time I'm digging my nails into the dirt and rock, thinking maybe I could survive. Only I can't hold on, so I fall again and wake up right before I hit the ground."

Slowly walking beside her, at her speed, he ponders the depth of her dream, that feeling of being out of control, and that reminds him: "I had this one reoccurring dream," he says, and she looks up at him with eyes that listen. "I was kidnapped, taken into a van by a nasty man with enormous hands, and there was one moment where I could take his gun but chickened out at first, then a few dreams later, I took it but couldn't fire it. He grabbed me before I could. It kept happening that way until I woke up one night and wrote down my own ending. The next time I had the dream I shot him right between the eyes. No more nightmare. See, you're the creator of your dreams, so rewrite them with better endings."

She shows interest in his advice, but her cynical side takes over, thinking positive thinking never worked for her before, then pauses to readjust her grip on the cane.

He doesn't know how long she can walk, but that's the goal, to get her leg accustomed to longer durations. Today's plan is to get to the cafe on the corner and come back, but the intensifying wind provides an occasional headwind that slows her progress. She holds onto him for support as they advance one step at a time. And knowing her tenacity, he wonders if he'll have to be the one to decide it's time to turn back, or else he might have to carry her home.

Nearly to the cafe, she cannot push against the wind any longer, so as he steers her to turn around, a gust whips in like the devil, playing mischief to the world outside their bubble. Money flies from the hand of a man paying his tab at the cafe. And one of the man's twenty-dollar bills swirls into their fishbowl, swirling around before landing on her ankle. Carney watches her scoop down to pick it up, reminding him of how she did that at the casino.

"Good to see nothing's changed," he says, laughing a little under his breath.

"What?" she asks innocently.

He knows she's no dummy, she heard every word, but she's only now realizing that he saw her pick up that old Cowboy's hundred dollar bill.

She doesn't know if she should be flattered or ashamed. She's never thought much about it, or whether it was right to or not. She hasn't had the luxury, and the philosophy of ethics isn't widely discussed between street dwellers and vagabonds.

Seeing that he slightly embarrassed her, he wraps his arms around her and guides her back down the boardwalk. He wants her to know he accepts her for who she is, and he doesn't want her to be someone she's not, of course, unless role-play is in order, but then says, "I'm not a big fan of the floral."

"Really?" she asks, finding it more comfortable to walk with the wind in their favor.

"Yeah," he goes on, "I prefer your leather and lace."

She forces a smile, hoping that it is a flirtatious joke because she is both leather and lace and floral cotton. She hopes he sees that side of her, but if he doesn't, it's only her fault for not telling him. Or maybe it's her fault for not living the floral cotton life enough for people to see that side of her. So caught up in her head and her walking, she forgets herself and stops at Mona's blue tent.

She calls out to her, "Mona?"

To his shock, a disheveled woman in braids peeks her face out of the tent. Her eyes wide with fright before smiling when she recognizes Pru.

Pru hands her the twenty-dollar bill and says, "Finder's givers, the wind delivers."

"Thanks, Pru," Mona says before disappearing back into her tent with a slight nod hello to Carney.

Inside his head, he is laughing hysterically, figuring, of course, Pru would be on a name-to-name basis with the homeless woman, the birds of a feather that they are.

He guides Pru around the encampment, dodging a young woman with a respirator mask, and they look to each other and communicate without even speaking the peculiarity of such behavior. Then watching the person until she's a few houses down the boardwalk, they slowly go up the stairs to Carney's front door.

"How's your leg feeling?" he asks.

"My leg feels like going to the bedroom to put on something a little more your style," she says flirtatiously. "Give me a minute?"

"Absolutely," he says, holding the door for her to enter.

Following her inside, he shuts the door, but he can't shake the eerie feeling of what he just saw. As much as he'd like to brush off her neighborliness as nothing because trust to him is better done than said, he's starting to wonder if he should. There are too many questions clinging to the walls of his brain. When did she get on a first-name basis with the homeless woman? Why didn't she tell him?

He imagines a hypothetical scenario where there is a setup between her and the homeless camp to steal all of his possessions and leave him broken-hearted. He imagines reacting to it, and it offends her, causing a scene that could result in her leaving. Then he asks himself, would this really offend him if she were a regular girl, not a drifter? Maybe he would be less concerned and even consider it a generous act to give away her found money. But his mind gets the better of him, and he goes to the bookshelf, pulling down Hemingway's *The Old Man and the Sea.*

Flipping through the pages, first quick and then slowly before turning it upside down and shaking it. No hidden money. *What are you doing?!?* He yells at himself. *This is that self-destructive shit she was talking about.* Reminding himself that he has to love all the things about her, that in the future, this will be the thing they laugh about most. Maybe he could even purposely leave money for her and leave her hints for where to find it, like a treasure hunt.

There's a loud banging at the front door!

"Who the fuck?" Carney says to himself while putting the book back on the shelf. Then going to the door, he opens it only to see it's his rebel pack from the cigar bar.

"There he is! Our friend who's forgotten us," Danny exclaims, barging in.

"Let us in, lover boy. Where is she?" Mark says in another one of his loud sports jackets, carving a path between the guys to enter.

"We brought beer!" Rocco and Diaz shout in unison and laugh at that.

They filter in, popping beers, putting Carney in a difficult position. Does he, or how does he kick them out? Will Pru think that he invited them over?

"Oh, shit," hollers Danny, "there's a bed in your living room."

"Are you making use of it?" Millennial asks, half laughing under his breath while looking at his phone as if nothing transpired between the two of them, and Carney almost loses his head.

"She here? Bring her out!" Mark calls out after lighting a cigar and handing his lighter to Rocco.

Danny hands a beer to his long lost buddy, and Carney nods in return, deciding to let go of what he can't control and go with where the wind is blowing him. He gestures his head in Mark's direction and asks Danny, "How's it going?"

Danny shrugs, troubled.

"We start pre-production next week," Mark interjects, noticing the exchange.

"No, we don't," Danny insists, revealing an underlying attitude toward the whole project.

Carney raises a brow. "Sounds like you two have a lot to talk about." Then finally acknowledging the smoke, Carney pleads, "Guys, I don't smoke in my place anymore."

"Seriously?" Diaz says, holding his cigar in mid-air but not in a hurry to extinguish it.

"Bro, you're fucking with us, right?" Rocco insists.

Millennial takes a big puff and blows it without any discretion, a slap in Carney's face.

Carney slaps back, "Did you not listen to what I just fuckin' said?!"

The guys go quiet, knowing what could go down. Millennial has been preaching his side of the Scott Manford story, and the guys don't know what's true. Although Carney doesn't know they know; he is preparing for a fight if it comes to that. But before Carney could act upon his new house rule, out walks Pru. Even with her cane, she looks sexy, walking the hallway like a runway, in a black silk robe showing her stockings held up by a garter belt.

"Just what every girl wants, a smokey entrance," she says, posing like an old-time movie star at the entrance to the living room.

Everyone looks, eyes wide open and speechless.

CHAPTER TWENTY TWO

"Holy shit," Marks blurts out, recognizing Pru from the mansion party where she was a nude art piece, but she doesn't recognize him. In a way, it's as if she's on a stage, unable to see beyond the lights.

"We weren't expecting company," Carney says.

He had no idea she would be walking out dressed the way she is, or hardly dressed is more accurate, but he holds back his shock and plays it off. Mostly, because she is his Penny character come to life.

"So you want us to leave, is what you're saying?" Danny challenges Carney.

"No, come sit at the table," Pru insists. "I'm not going to turn down an opportunity to meet Carney's friends."

She walks toward the table, oozing sex and putting more weight on her leg than she's used to; even though each step is agonizingly painful, she wants to look beautiful and tenacious. The guys look at Carney with their big googly eyes, giving him props, but he's got all eyes on Pru, wondering what her next move will be. He doesn't even catch Mark giving her a wink as she passes by.

The wink seems oddly familiar to her, and she begins to remember him and his insidious way of insinuating she was someone she's not. Her worlds collide, and she worries that this won't go over smoothly, but she stays strong and in-character, and on the way to the table, she takes a detour into the privacy of the kitchen where she can pop a pill. She hid one in a ball of foil inside the utensil drawer, the place where hardly used kitchen gadgets go to die. After swallowing it with faucet water, she grabs an ashtray Carney stored with the mixing bowls and serving dishes, taking it with her into the living room to the big table by the window.

"Anyone got a cigar for me?" she asks, sitting at the table.

They all pull out their cigars.

"Put them away," Carney says. "I got her."

He grabs two cigars from his humidor while the guys come to the table like a bunch of carnivorous animals trying to sit like gentlemen. Pru crosses her legs and rests them on the seat next to her to elevate. Carney sits on the other side of her leg like a protector, giving her the cut cigar. She puts it in her mouth while keeping a watchful eye on the enemy as Mark sits across the table from her. Carney takes note of her sideways glance as she puffs and puffs, getting a good burn.

Everything Pru does is erotic to the guys, and they try not to be obvious as they gawk at her. Carney knows the feeling. She doesn't have to be in lingerie to be sexy. The subtleties of her movements, her quiet strength, it's hypnotic. She's a natural. Carney sees now how she could never be a Mona. She has way too much game. Even with her scarred up leg, Penny has so many possibilities—his story plays in his head.

With her cigar finally lit, she focuses on Diaz. "So Diaz, how's the movie version of your life story going?"

Diaz laughs, asking, "How do you know I'm Diaz?"

"Call it an educated guess," she says, giving an eye to Carney.

"Smart and beautiful," Rocco interjects. "Have any friends?" He is not the only one who wants to know. Diaz looks pretty eager, too. Carney questions what this game of hers is really all about.

She takes a slow puff, calculating her response. "Girls, as friends, are really future enemies masquerading as allies," she says. Giving eyes to Carney, reminding him of who said it first and why, and also to reassure him she hasn't forgotten. He acknowledges their little secret by giving her a sly smile. He's willing to let her play out this hand or whatever she's planning. He knows she is on his side.

"So, no," she says, turning her gaze to Rocco, whom she's never met before. "Sorry, Rocco."

Rocco's eyes widen with another level of excitement. "I love this girl!"

Millennial laughs under his breath, looking at his phone. Everyone ignores him like they usually do, all but for Carney and Pru. She wishes she could reach her hand to Carney's heart and heal the indignation he's feeling inside right now. Having heard Carney yell at Millennial before she walked out of the bedroom, she's concerned his self-destructive switch has already been activated, and there's nothing that can be done.

Carney takes it as an insult that Millennial is in his house after lying to him the way he did. He wonders if the guys know, and a part of him wants to believe they don't, but he's not a fool anymore. So he can only assume Millennial told his side, or whatever lie he peddles.

"So, how's the leg?" Rocco continues the conversation with Pru.

For self-satisfying reasons, she'd love to tell him how it really is. That she's received a new limb without a manual, and the constant pain only reminds her that she doesn't know how to operate it yet. That she swings from feeling agony to defeat on such a consistent basis, she would be distraught if it weren't for Carney. He keeps her motivated. Not only because she wants to show him that she can regain her ability to walk without a cane, but because she desires to perform daily acts of kindness and keep up the morale of the house. But instead, she declares, "Happy to have a leg."

"Let me tell you, this girl strapped a board to her leg so she wouldn't have to walk like a pirate," Carney defends her strength with a sharpness they're not used to and looks at her proudly. "Straightened her right up."

"There's nothing I wouldn't do to get what I want," she says matter-of-factly, looking back at Carney.

Mark looks on with extra judgment. "I bet."

"You bet what?!" Carney's quick to confront him, and Mark doesn't bounce back. The tension is thick, and the smoke is heavy.

Rocco looks at Danny. "You got nothing to say? I thought you got your boy Carney's back, but now Mark's directing you in a film, you're all quiet?"

Danny gets pissed. "I don't fucking know her," he says and turns his back to Carney. "He hasn't talked to us in weeks."

Millennial interjects, "Danny, wasn't it your idea to come here?"

Carney stares down Millennial and snaps, "Why the fuck are you here?" Millennial sits tongue-tied, and all eyes are on him. Carney continues, "I was determined to let this go and be cool, but you only remind me of how uncool you really are. You have no right being here after the betrayal you played."

"Betrayal?" Diaz asks.

Carney replies, "He straight-up lied to me, not only to get me to do free work but put me in a bad spot with an old friend."

"That's not what he told us," Mark interjects.

"No, he lied," Diaz says. "He's a liar. Carney's right. He's got no right being here." Diaz looks directly into Millennial's eyes when he says, "Get the fuck out."

"This is bullshit!" Millennial insists. But the guys just stare, so he knows he's done. He throws his cigar into the ashtray without putting it out.

Diaz grabs ahold of his arm. "You've got no respect. Put that out." Then releases his arm, and Millennial does what he says and dabs out his cigar. Then they all watch as Millennial turns toward the door, and with nothing more to say, out he goes.

"Good riddance," Rocco says.

To release the tension, Pru brandishes a Mae West imitation. Saying, "I get it, I'm like the new animal at the zoo," the guys turn their attention to her, "but soon my mystique will wear off, and he'll kick me out on my hinny to fend for myself. Won't you, doll?"

Carney laughs while brandishing his own old-timey accent, saying, "I don't know about that. I'm kinda fond of that hinny and that precious brain it's attached to."

The rebel pack looks at each other, not believing what they're seeing.

Danny throws up his hands. "Aw, we lost him! Carney's gone."

The guys laugh.

Rocco does the sign of the cross in Carney's direction. "God rest his soul. He will be missed."

The guys laugh some more. Including Carney, but he thinks it's funny because it's the truth; he is gone, and he might never be back.

"That's funny," Mark says sarcastically. "Especially because of who she is. Or is it what she does? No, who she does."

The laughter dies, and all eyes are on the Carney-and-Mark stare down. Until Carney pounces from his seat to unleash his angst on Mark's face, but before he does, Rocco takes hold of his arm with the force like he's stopping a train.

"It's not worth it, man," Rocco urges him.

Carney pulls back and shouts, "That's it. Everyone get the fuck out!"

Mark stands to leave first, saying to Pru, "Catch you on the fly, Eyeballs."

Carney clenches his fists again, but Rocco holds him back until Mark is out the door.

"I said, everyone!" Carney tells them, waving his arms around madly, herding his cigar toking brood out.

"Hey, he's always been an asshole," Danny says, trying to calm his friend. "Every crew has one."

Diaz grabs Carney by the shoulder and pulls him in to say, "Call me if you need me." Carney nods, and Rocco grabs the beer.

"Thanks," Carney says to Rocco.

Rocco nods, saying, "Take care of your girl. We love you, bro." He's the last to leave and shuts the door behind him.

Carney takes a moment to bottle the rage inside of him. What did he expect? He knew she was no angel, but is it possible she's duplicitous on top of being a thief?

He walks back with a strange calm, but inside he's a volcano ready to blow. Mark's no stranger to the working girls of Hollywood, so Carney can only assume Pru is one.

She's got her legs up on the table now, her silk robe split open slightly, giving him a taste of the black lace teddy underneath, and her cold demeanor tells him she's ready for a fight.

He circles the living room, thinking they were just about to have a fun, playful evening together, and now this. He's been nothing but trusting, patient, and accepting. It angers him that there's still so much crippling unknown about her, and little by little, she's letting him fall in love with her knowing what he doesn't know. He begins to fear that everything about her is a lie, that she's singing for her supper, and he's just the sucker.

"I don't even know who you are right now," he lets out.

"Look how easy you take the hook."

"Oh, but your hook is just fine?" he exclaims, his blood boiling. "You have your sharp claws so deeply embedded in me I can't even see it happening."

She smiles, choosing to take that as a compliment but wonders if she told him everything about her past, would this be happening now? She never intended to remain a mystery. Her intention was always for him to get to know the real her beyond all the red flags and deal-breakers. It's inconvenient, not to mention uncomfortable, to bring up her past and the many couches she's stayed on, and all the odd jobs she's had. She figures he should know her essence by now, so the real test is, what does he do now? Will he let his judgment override what he knows in his heart about her? Watching him open the slider to air out the smoke, she wonders what he's thinking as he stands there looking out at the boardwalk and beyond.

"I've been so worried you'd heal and fly away I didn't even see your game," he states so frigidly.

Her heart aches, seeing how quickly he could turn on her. She closes her robe tighter, feeling the invasive air from outside give her goosebumps.

"Don't do this," she warns.

"How can I trust anything you've ever said?"

"Because it's the truth."

He laughs.

"I was a live model at a party," she confesses with a serious tone, hoping to turn this around, "and he took me for one of the other girls that work for my boss."

"Now there's a boss," he says, going for a bottle of whiskey in the liquor cabinet. "Just keeps getting better."

"You're pressing the self-sabotage button again."

"Oh, you think you've got me all figured out. You've said this more than once now. Maybe you're the one who self-sabotages," he fires a shot. "It's not bad luck. It's you."

His words are like daggers to her soul. Enraged and hurt, she stands up, her hand shaky on her cane. "Predictable," she says with her voice cracking. "Blame me. Write me as a villain and cast me out. That was your plan this whole time, wasn't it? God forbid you acknowledge any real feelings for me! That's too dangerous."

He nods and walks into the bedroom, leaving her unsettled. She worries this could be the beginning of the end, that she might have to prepare for sleeping somewhere else tonight. Then he reappears from the bedroom in an overcoat and heads toward the door.

"I need some air," he says, heading out into the darkness.

She goes to the side window in the kitchen and watches him walk briskly toward the alleyways. He has been her everything for so long now. It is strange to suddenly feel like he is a stranger, but she has to start wrapping her head around that idea. In a flash of time, he could become nothing but a memory, someone she recovered from a broken leg with.

On the boardwalk, Mark looks up from his heated conversation with Danny to see Carney disappearing down the alley.

While inside, Pru hobbles into Carney's walk-in closet with sadness in her eyes. She figures she'll go back to Doug's tonight; she still has stuff there. Knowing it will be a blowout flight when Carney returns, she packs her things into bags now. When the moment comes, she wants to be ready. And it's always so difficult to pack during an argument.

Suddenly, the doorbell rings, startling her. *Did Carney forget his keys?* She goes to the door suspiciously, asking,

"Who's there?" No answer, only the sound of heavy feet impatiently waiting. It's not Carney, she knows he wouldn't play games like that.

She could try to look out the side window, but she's not opening the door for anyone but Carney. So she goes back to the bedroom closet because hidden in one of her shoe boxes is Carney's gun, only being right-handed, that's the hand she uses to hold her cane, so she tries walking with the cane in her left hand, it's more difficult, but she manages. Eventually, she gets to the door. She puts her ear to it to see if whoever is still there but only hears silence. She lets out a sigh of relief.

Her leg, however, is not relieved at all. It's throbbing with pain. She's put her wounded limb through quite a day, especially since she can feel the pain while on a pill. She goes into the now dark kitchen to see if there is another pill, only to be scared half to death. Mark is sitting at the table with his legs folded like a creep.

"So, what's your con?"

"How did you get in?"

"Sliding door."

She looks. It's open.

"Carney's coming right back," she insists, but it's more like she hopes.

"He ain't coming back for a while. I saw the look on his face. He's going to walk and talk this one all night. He's got that paranoia that explodes upon impact, and I hit him good."

She points the gun at him. "Get out. Now!"

"Not without what I came for." He stands up and takes a step toward her. "Agree to make me partner, and I'll leave."

"This isn't what you think it is," she cocks the trigger.

He holds his distance a few feet away. "You're good. Lie to him all you want, but I'm like you. We can be real with each other. You need me. That boy's paranoid as fuck. You're dead as a doornail to him unless I tell him any different."

She grins because Mark's deflection only tells her that he needs her, not the other way around.

"You feel small. That's why you're puffing out your chest like you are." She un-clicks the trigger and lowers the gun, "but you don't have to. No one cares. Instead of instilling fear, you should try inducing love. It's a far better currency."

"You do you. I'll do me," Mark says, taking a step toward her. "You may think you're safe in his expensive house, that his money is a wall protecting you from who you really are." Another step. "Let me tell you..." He comes at her with both arms out like a lion, one hand reaching for her throat and the other for the gun. She tries to raise the gun to him, but their arms collide, knocking the gun across the kitchen floor. She tries to push him off, but he is too strong. He holds her down onto the kitchen counter by her throat.

"I can get to you in this world and the next," he hisses, "Doug's house, or wherever you end up."

She knows he's only trying to scare her because if he were trying to kill her, he'd be squeezing her throat. She's not sitting pretty, though, because his thumb is digging into the gap underneath her jaw, just below her chin, and she's locked down, not going anywhere. But her left hand is still holding onto her cane, so she flings it up fast and hard and hits him in the head. He squints like a fly is bothering him and, out of anger, squeezes her throat, causing her to gasp for air. She hits him harder, and this time she aims for the ear. *Whup!* His grip loosens out of reflex, and she whacks him in the throat. He releases his grip, coughing and gasping for air. She stumbles to get upright, and he looks at her like he's gonna kill her. Needing to get to the gun fast, she hobbles a few steps with the help of the counter and then leaps for it, and her outstretched hand grabs the Colt's handle. She swings around, pointing the gun, ready to defend, but he's not there. The front door is open, and he's gone.

CHAPTER TWENTY THREE

Carney walks, caught in a struggle with his thoughts like there's an equation inside his head he can't solve. Thinking back to Vegas, he wonders if she were really there as a working girl instead of what she said, going to a friend's wedding. Why does he care so much? If she were honest that first night, he wouldn't have minded but so much has transpired since then. Their relationship is different, he is different, and he can't let this equation go unsolved.

Then, remembering at the hospital when she said she didn't have any friends, and now there's a boss, is everything she tells him a lie, or is he looking for the lie to escape his feelings for her? Because even as he is thinking this out, his gut tells him he's wrong. She is an enigma, after all, so there's a chance she's telling the truth. For, her-truth is unbelievable. Then he recalls her Vegas story when she said she wouldn't be a stripper because she couldn't do the lap dancing. There was no reason for her to lie to him then. The story was sordid enough without her censoring only that part, so common sense tells him she's not one of those girls.

He's solved it. She may be an odd darling, but she's not duplicitous. He can't have the story go that way, and in truth, she's lived an unimaginable life. Her past is her past, stories birthed from pain, and he loves that about her.

Looking up, he sees flashing lights from a squad of police cars on the boardwalk outside his house, and cops are taping off the scene. Walking past some neighbors gathering, he overhears someone was shot, dead.

Carney goes around to get a better look. A man is facedown on the concrete, and blood pools around him. The man is wearing the same loud pattern sport jacket that Mark had on. It is Mark. He knows instantly, this will not look good for them. That's when he looks up toward the house and sees Pru's face looking through the open drapes of the sliding glass door. He can't tell if she is looking at the crime scene or looking at him until she changes her gaze to lock eyes with his.

He needs to get to her and see what she knows. Getting through the growing crowd, he stumbles to make it to his front door. Coming in, he sees Pru standing by the patio door, delirious with the gun hanging in her hand.

"What did you do?" he asks, inching toward her slowly because of the gun before realizing it's his father's gun.

"He broke in and attacked me," she motions to her throat. "He tried to blackmail me to steal your money, and I had to fight him off. I hit him a few times, and that's when I went for the gun..."

"Give me the gun," he interjects, with a soft authoritative tone, and takes the gun delicately from her shaking hand. He never liked Mark, and he's not sad that he's gone. What would make him miserable is if she had to go away for this. "Come here," he says, pulling her into his chest as the flashing lights pulsate through the glass. Then wonders if they're both doomed, two dreamers with bad nightmares like two gamblers with bad luck.

"It'll be okay. Don't worry. We have to stick together," he says while thinking of a plan and making a list in his head. The first thing is to call Hops, tie up any loose ends, and then tells her, "In the morning, I'll call the lawyer. He'll make this disappear." He holds her, thinking about where problems could arise. Figuring which character in her old world is the most risk to her, it hits him. *That boss of hers.* If this is going to work, he needs to cover all the bases.

"I didn't shoot him," she says, needing to clarify, but he doesn't acknowledge her. He rubs her back, comforting her, and it suddenly occurs to her to ask, "Where were you?"

He grunts a little under his breath, reluctantly, and admits, "Thinking about this boss of yours."

"Doug?" she asks.

His eyes stare off into nothing, obsessed. "Yeah, Doug."

CHAPTER TWENTY FOUR

In the violet light of the sunrise, Carney glides through the streets of Los Angeles, windows down, thoughts on overdrive. He didn't sleep a wink last night while Pru's words echo around in his head. "Doug's just a friend. He lets me crash at his house sometimes and store some stuff there." Carney knows no guy lets a girl crash unless he's interested in her or has some other ulterior motive, and Carney's determined to find out which it is. He doesn't want any loose ends from her past coming up to bite them going forward because he considers her a part of his life now. They are wound together by tragedy.

Turning left up La Brea, he lets the Nova rumble through the neighborhood, waking up the bar-hoppers and the late risers. As he gains elevation, following the Maps app's directions, the property tax increases as well, and he tries to speculate what kind of guy Doug is. From what Pru told him, he's a bit of a hustler, party promotions and event services, or whatever that's code for, and as he pulls to a stop in front of the house, he lets his muscle car idle while he assesses this hustler's homestead. The guy either can't afford a gardener or is cheap. *Cheap and lazy,* he thinks. Maybe this guy rents. He surely doesn't respect his neighbors or neighborhood by having such an eyesore.

The street's on a thirty-degree angle, so Carney turns the steering wheel to curb the tires and fires off the engine. Before getting out of the car, he adjusts his dad's gun, concealed in the back of his jeans, and loosens his shirt around it.

Stepping out onto the asphalt with his big black engineer boots, thankful for his steel toes in times like these, he swings shut the door and struts up the weeded walkway, each step aggressive and with purpose, and knocks on the heavy wooden door. Looking around while he waits, he sees the windows drawn, and although the neighborhood is quiet, he can hear something from inside, maybe a girl. The door opens, a groggy and disheveled Doug stands in a bathrobe and loafers looking confused.

Carney gets right to it. "You Doug?"

"You a cop?" he answers a question with a question.

"Not a cop," Carney pops off, starting to put some pieces together already, feeling confident that his first assessment of Pru wasn't too far off, that she does come from a dark and desperate world. "I'm here to pick up Pru's belongings," he continues.

"Pru?" Doug rubs his chin, trying to recall who Pru could be. He knows so many girls, by so many different names, and then remembers Rui also goes by Pru. "You mean Rui," Doug corrects him, with an inflated chest.

Carney's not surprised. "Sure."

Doug folds his arms with speculation. "Why isn't she here? Who are you to her?"

Carney's calm and curt, explaining, "Look, man, I'm here to get her stuff. We got into a motorcycle accident, and I've been taking care of her."

"What? This is a joke."

There's nothing funny about Carney's disposition. "Do I look like I'm joking?"

Carney forces out his phone to show him a photo of Pru with her bandaged leg just after the accident. Doug's mood changes entirely, and he opens the door to let him in. Carney enters the dilapidated mansion and looks around. It's dark and musty, bare of furnishings, and seeing the porn play on the living room tv, he wonders if he interrupted something.

Doug sees him looking at the tv and says, "Don't mind that. It plays here like background music."

Carney isn't shy about showing his judgment and gets right to it. "So, where's her stuff?"

"Whoa, man, you still haven't said who you are to her. Rui's like family to me."

Carney wants to maintain his anonymity, so he speaks in general terms. "I'm her boyfriend."

Doug goes to the couch opening a box and removing a small baggie filled with cocaine, aware that it might not be Carney's thing.

"You want?" Doug offers.

Carney's quick to reject, "No."

Doug smirks, knowing he's figured him right, and, in a sick way, he takes pleasure in exposing the fractured worlds they live in. To a druggie, the divide is apparent between the doers and the ones who don't, and it goes the other way too.

"Boyfriend, huh. That's dangerous business," Doug stokes the fire. "Good luck with that."

"I'm not dying anytime soon," Carney insists.

While cutting up a line with a razor blade, Doug challenges him to see who knows her better. "So she told you about them?" Them, referring to her past boyfriends.

Carney has no intentions of giving over their private conversations. But if he doesn't say anything, it will look like he didn't know. He stands firm waiting for this pompous performance to be through and suffices him with a short, "Yep."

"Don't believe the last one was a suicide," Doug warns, looking to Carney to see if the shock has landed on his face. It hasn't, so he continues, "The family thinks she pushed him off that roof and took his money, cash laying around the house and stuff."

Carney will not be pushed into conspiracy theories. He's heard too many about his own family, and they are merely false fires meant to wreak havoc. Although, the truth is that Pru could have taken that money. He knows she likes to take money that's not hers, but the dead guy's family doesn't know her as he does. She's not a predator, like a tarantula she'd only defend if she were threatened. The girl's got to survive. For a moment, he wonders if this dead guy's family will be a problem for them moving forward, but upon second thought, he's not worried. People act strange when they're in grief, especially if it's an untimely death.

Carney's silence feeds Doug's ego. "So, you don't know?" Doug insinuates.

"No, I know the truth," Carney lies.

Doug sees right through him and prods on, "The cops were looking into it for a while, so be careful, man."

Carney smirks to play along as a notification appears on his phone. He reads, "Murder on Venice Beach boardwalk last night." He's pulled away for a moment, thinking about last night. If she's capable of killing Mark, all be it self-defense, she could be capable of other so-called self-defense ordeals, like these exes of hers. The human spirit is capable of almost anything under the right circumstances.

He remembers her telling him the second guy's story and how defensive she got when he asked her what she did next. It could be a tell that she had something to do with it. Or maybe she didn't want to talk about it anymore and got defensive. Perhaps, she'll tell him one day when she trusts him more once she realizes that he's not going anywhere because what he has with her is made of stone, not sand, and he's betting on it.

Doug finally snorts one of the lines. "You got a name, boyfriend?"

Carney's had about enough of this guy's game. "Look, you say she's like family, but you haven't even asked how she's doing." He cuts with the bullshit and gets real, "So let's not act like we're gonna see each other again."

"Well then," Doug snorts his final line, "don't let the past get between you two."

"Just show me her stuff."

Doug puts away his drugs with a mischievous smile, fixes his bathrobe, and rises to the occasion, guiding Carney down the long hallway.

"I don't keep a room for everyone," Doug whispers like he's telling him a secret, "but she's special." He smiles creepily. "But I don't have to tell you that."

Doug stops walking, expecting a response, but Carney senses the attack and holds back. Then Doug opens a door. It's dusty and vacant like a tomb, and scraps of her things lay on a single bed.

"I like my girls to sleep in their own room," Doug postures. "Giving them a sense of their own independence is important, you know, so they don't get clingy."

Carney fires him a look like he wants to shoot him dead right there but instead chooses to go into the room to get this over and done. He knows what kind of guy Doug is. He is a scheming, self-serving asshole, and he's glad Pru had the common sense not to be with this guy but feels sorry that she was ever in a position of needing him. He could see how this jerk would take advantage of that.

"Her stuff's in the closet," Doug barks.

Carney's cautious opening the closet doors, for he doesn't know what he'll find. It's another layer he's unveiling. It's one thing to hear about her past and another to see the evidence. He folds open the white-wood slatted door and takes inventory with his mind. Black tight-fitting dresses hang loosely over bags filled with what appears to be more clothes, or some type of costume, and knee-high boots, stiletto boots, and high heels. Relieved to see it is only clothes, he can imagine what kind of girl she was here, influenced to use her sexuality for monetary gain, and it heightens his dislike for Doug. He begins to clear out the closet of her belongings, assessing how many trips to his car, probably two or three, and fills his arms up to his neck for trip one.

While waiting for Carney to finish, Doug leans up against the hallway wall looking at his phone with his robe agape to show off his manhood that appears large in his male thong. As if that would intimidate Carney; anything looks big when you stuff it into a sack and pull the string.

On Carney's last trip, he looks around the room one last time to make sure he's got everything. Nothing more in the closet, so he looks under the bed, nothing. He opens the bedside drawer and discovers a notebook. Scribbles on the front don't tell him anything, so he turns the pages only to realize that it's poetry. He stops at a poem titled "Sin City Summer" and decides to read it. He looks to the door for Doug, but he's not visible, so he sits down on the bed and dives in, hearing Pru's voice speak inside his head.

Sin City Summer

This desert sand is quick, devoured me whole,
Spitting me out in hopeful pieces,
Pieces that cannot exist to function minus the rest.
The transition to this position, broke down desert,
Pathetic ruin, dented destiny now denied.
I'm dog bitten, money forbidden,
My morality now in question.
Who and what am I?
This fucking fantasy, I lay, then disobey,
And pray for a hero today.

Gaming hearts for a future,
Inside I know the truth here,
And yet existing unsustainably without fear.
Every stare impairs and makes well aware,
The insecurity I bare, yet somehow somewhere,
I'm losing the will to care.

Trying and trying,
But feeding only this want for dying,
Wanting now for this getting to be got,
And hoping for you to untie this knot.
Take me from this unfortunate spot.

He rolls up her notebook and stuffs it inside one of her boots. Then he shovels the remainder of her items into his arms. Cradling the last of her past, he heads for the front door.

"Hey, look at this," Doug says, keeping him there and holds out his phone like he's got something special to show him.

Carney doesn't want to stop or look, but Doug forces the picture in his face. It's Pru, naked with a huge bag of drugs.

"Look how happy she is here."

That's it. Carney drops his armful and punches him in the gut, knocking the wind out of him, and forces him to the floor. He doesn't stop there. He pins Doug's head to the hardwood and takes his phone.

"You don't give a fuck about her, you fucking loser," Carney says, releasing his anguish. Then deletes the picture. "And if anyone comes around asking about her, you don't know shit about her past. And I was never here. Or I'm going to have to come back here and put a bullet in your head. You get me?!"

Doug's in no position to disagree. "Hey, this is no *True Romance* situation here, dude. We're cool." Carney releases his hold, grabs her items, and leaves.

Walking to the car, he wonders if Pru thinks of him as a hero like the one she spoke of in her poem. Certainly, he believes he can be, especially if he gets her out of this mess. He knows if the cops haven't arrived yet, they soon will be, and if there's anyone who knows how to get her out of this, it's the McMorris' family attorney. He's cleaned the muck from the gutters of many in these Hollywood hills.

As he drives back down the way he came, he puts his earbuds in and says, "Siri, call The Wolf."

CHAPTER TWENTY FIVE

Pru wakes up to the sound of sizzling bacon, then looks to Carney's side of the bed that hasn't been slept in and dreads the misery she's caused. All this wouldn't have happened had she not come into his life. Yet, she propels herself forward and out of bed to encounter what's coming to her.

Hearing toast popping up from the toaster, she walks with her cane toward the kitchen, expecting to see a frantic Carney cooking breakfast, but she's startled to see a man she's never met before. She recognizes him right away from *Walking Alone,* as well as his many other films.

"You're, uh, you're..." She's still waking up and finding that her words are coming slowly.

"Carney's godfather, Hops Gardner. I'm an old buddy of Mitch's," he says as he taps on the *Walking Alone* poster with his knuckle.

Thinking he looks amiable enough, but his mood is tense, so as thrilled as she would be to meet him under other conditions, these are different circumstances. Then she wonders what Carney told him but assumes he is aware of the night's events. Only what are they? She is still confused.

"Where's Carney?" she asks, sitting anxiously at the kitchen table.

Hops serves her a plate of scrambled eggs, bacon, and toast, getting a good look at her. He expected a beauty, and there's no doubt that she is. Even without makeup, her bone structure gives the impression that she is, and her slender frame has a beautiful way of carrying her muscles. She could be an athlete if she wanted. Or, he ponders, she could prowl the sons of famous actors, like a panther waiting to pounce.

"He's protecting his assets," he says. "Which includes you too now, the reason I'm here, to keep anyone from asking any incriminating questions." Hops sits down with his own plate of bacon and a side of eggs and gets right into it, "Let me tell you, the next forty-eight hours is going to be a heavyweight battle on you both."

"I'm nothing but bad luck. I'll leave if it'll stop all this."

"I bet you would," he says judgmentally, "but you'd do more damage leaving, so stay put, little darlin'."

She attempts to dig for more information. "I just don't understand what is going on," she says so innocently she sounds like a little girl.

Hops looks her over, doubting she is really that naive. "Where did you grow up?" he asks, hoping to figure her out a bit.

She finishes a bite, exclaiming, "North of Santa Barbara, near Ravens Ranch."

"Really?" His eyes widen with recognition. "I know that ranch." He smiles out of the corner of his mouth. "Chips and Paula sold me a horse a ways back. Good people."

"The best," she proclaims, noticing he's loosening up. Feeding the fire in her favor, she paints the picture for him, "I would ride my bike over there when I was a kid and spend hours brushing the horses and braiding their manes, even if the horse was a boy," she giggles.

Hops imagines her as a kid with her pigtails and enthusiasm. He had a niece who was like that, and then she grew up. Boys became her focus, and she lost her way. He would have stepped in, in some wise uncle capacity, but she lived in Texas with his sister, although every time she comes for a visit, that little ranch girl would ignite in her eyes again.

"You and Carney should come to visit my ranch when this is all done."

"You have a ranch?" she asks pleasantly.

"It's no Ravens Ranch. It's a small spread in Rolling Hills, on the Palos Verdes peninsula. Though there is a trail where you can see the ocean."

Imagining it, she feels a calm come over her, but the event that brought them together today can't escape her mind. She thinks now is the time to confess her truth to Hops and see where the cards fall. "I have to tell you," she looks him dead in his eyes and says, "I didn't kill him."

He listens, eating a strip of bacon.

She goes on, "I think Carney thinks I did it." She lays down her napkin on the table like a deck of cards, waiting for him to tell her what to do.

He only nods, then pats her hand comfortingly like it will be all right, but she doesn't feel comforted. She needs words, real words of assurance. But instead, she hears the garage door opening and closing. Any minute Carney will be coming in, so she looks to Hops again, but he's not concerned at all. He shovels a forkful of eggs into his mouth and *click* goes the door. In comes Carney with an armful of her belongings, quickly changing the mood.

"We gotta go. It's all set up," Carney voices with intensity as he zips into their bedroom to drop off her stuff.

She turns to face his general direction, asking, "What is?"

Carney doesn't answer. He comes into the kitchen like a steaming locomotive and hands his father's gun over to Hops.

"I'll get this back from you later."

"Where's the case?"

"I'll go get it."

Carney steams off toward the bedroom again, and Pru watches with confusion while Hops gets up to wrap the revolver in a dishtowel.

Carney comes back with the case, and she stands to stop him. "Wait. What just happened? Where were you?"

"You know where I was," he proclaims with a deep tone and direct eye contact.

When he asked for Doug's address last night, she assumed that's where he went, and now seeing her clothes from there, she knows that's where he was. Although, seeing his godfather wrap the gun in a towel, she imagines the worst and the many ways it could go down. But knowing the two of them, she figures Doug was an asshole, and Carney unloaded all his unsettled emotions into him. She wants to blurt-out, *did you shoot him? What are your plans for me? For us? Are we okay? Do you blame me?* But she settles on subtly, asking, "Everything okay?"

"Everything's fine," he says in a calmer tone. "He's not going to say anything about you. I made it real clear."

She's temporarily relieved, but as he ushers her into the bedroom to get dressed, her doubts and concerns flood her mind again. *What are your plans for me? For us? Do you blame me? Are we okay?*

CHAPTER TWENTY SIX

Pru rides shotgun, unsure of what Carney's plan is, only knowing that they're headed to the police station to make their statements. Although unsure of a lot right now, she knows that her statement might not match up with his, but that's the way it goes. Everyone's experience is different, even when it's the same. Perspective is everything, and out the passenger side window, her world blurs. And she reminds herself, in addition to being a passenger in his car, she's also a passenger in his life, going with the flow and awaiting instruction.

Spotting a large bird soaring above, as it dips down, she sees it's a pelican. Even though they're close to the beach, it still seems rare to see a pelican so far inland. She wonders if it's lost, and then thinking of the pelican's perspective, it gets her back to herself. All these years living couch to couch, she thought she was free, but now she sees the bars of her cage and ponders that everyone lives in their own version of a cage. She sees Carney's bars, built by his father's legacy, but the space between the bars is spacious, and it could be comfortable living for her there. She realizes freedom lives in the ability to choose your cage. A choice she thought she had until he walked in on her with the gun in her hand. What does he think happened? What happens after they give their statements? Does he still want to be with her? Men always look out for themselves, so will he tell the police she had his gun? If he tells them and she doesn't, it won't look good for her. Lying is an obstruction of justice. That could garner her up to five years in prison and fines she couldn't afford to pay.

Idling at a red light, he grabs ahold of her hand, interlacing his fingers in hers. The hairs on the back of her neck tingle from his touch. She looks to him with every drop of hope in her heart that everything will be all right.

He says, "My dad was nominated for three Oscars and won one," his eyes lock with hers, "but the best role he played had nothing to do with the movies. He had a stalker, nutty like *Play Misty For Me.*" The light turns green, and he puts the car into gear without removing his hand from hers. "This girl left cow hearts on our doorstep and bloody finger paintings on our windows." She listens as he navigates them around a slow car, looking at both her and the road like he's watching a game of tennis. "And one night she broke into our home and my dad shot her." He pauses before adding, "He killed her."

That's a hell of an ace! she thinks.

Recognizing that this is privy information, information that has been kept secret, she knows a lot of trust comes with that and wonders why he would tell her as her heart beats faster.

"Hops told me after my father died," he continues, "and now I'm telling you. I've never told anyone and will never tell anyone else, but the current situation dictates. Just know that in our family, normal rules don't apply.

No good will come from dragging our name through the dirt." He pulls into the Santa Monica Police Station, curving around to the underground lot. "You're not a bad person, and neither was my dad." He rolls down his window to take a parking ticket and waits to be clear of the gate before rolling it back up again. "You have to put on a performance of a lifetime. Convince them you didn't kill Mark. You have to believe you didn't do it. Go inward, find a truth within and let that live for the lie."

She wants to stop him and tell him this is all irrelevant. She didn't do it. She's innocent. Well, maybe not innocent, but she didn't kill him. Only, she said that to Carney last night. He obviously doesn't believe her. They never do.

He pulls into the handicap spot up front and lets go of her hand to hook the handicap placard on the rearview, but then he turns to her and says, "Luckily, for the most part, we're fairly innocent, victims even. You're recovering from an accident. You're in no condition. Make them feel that." What could she do? Nodding or other forms of agreeing seem to her like lying, so she squeezes his hand and listens. "They're going to deal some low cards because that's who they are. And this is important. The gun doesn't exist. You never had it." She nods to that, and he continues, "Be as you are with me." He assures her, "You play this game better than any of them." She wonders what he means by that, but then again, she realizes she is yet to understand his perspective. "I believe in you," he says before turning off the engine. "I love you."

She's shocked, hearing those words, *I love you?* Her first instinct is to doubt the validity, convince herself that he's laying it on thick to persuade her to perform, but that's her insecurity talking, the part of her that doesn't believe she's worthy of love.

He gets out of the car, so she opens her door, positions her cane, and pulls herself up on her feet, reminding herself to put weight on her bad leg because it's so easy for her to lean away from pain, and wishes she had another pain pill. She'll have to talk to Mona when they get back to the house—if they get back to the house because when she closes the car door, her reflection in the car window makes her worry that this could be the last image she has of herself before being arrested and taken to jail. And as she comes around the backside of the Nova, she notices through the back window that her notebook is on the backseat next to his computer bag.

"Is that my poetry book?"

"Yeah," he says, offering her his arm. "I drove up to Griffith Observatory this morning and read all your poems. They're outstanding."

Not believing her ears, she wonders if it's possible that she's been too hard on herself and that perhaps Carney really could love her?

CHAPTER TWENTY SEVEN

Carney sits alone in the Chief of Police's office after giving his statement directly to Chief Starr. The McMorris' family lawyer made that happen, but how far that privilege goes is uncertain. His father's fame garnered exceptional and unusual treatment when he was alive, but he's gone now, and Carney's concerned for Pru. They've been separated in different rooms for over an hour. He hopes it's a guy who's interrogating her. She'll tear him apart. He's sure of it.

In the interrogation room, Pru waits for Detective Young to return and release her. In the meantime, she stares down at the black and gray checkerboard floor, reflecting back to the same casino flooring that she strutted across when she had two perfect legs, at the Ellis Island Casino, where Carney came into her life. As she imagines her life, like a game on a chessboard, she wonders if she is winning or losing. If this moment is just another move on the board or if this is game over.

She rests her leg on the top of the table to increase her circulation. She was told it might be up to a year before her leg functions like normal, but she doubts normal is something she'll ever know. Even Carney's stable world is far from typical.

Facing the mirror, she wonders if anyone's watching on the other side. And going over her statement in her head, she assures herself that she said all she needed to say. Of course, she left out some details that could be used to incriminate her, like the gun, the fact that Mark snuck in through the sliding door, and diminished the physical attack to a simple disagreement. She wished she could have skipped that part altogether, but she had to say something. The rebel pack would tell their story, and Mark's accusations needed closure.

She looked deep into Detective Young's eyes and concluded, "It's he said against she said and he's dead. While I'm very much alive," and Detective Young seemed convinced before exiting the room.

She tries to recall if she saw any homeless on the boardwalk after the gunshots, but she can't be sure. Figuring she'll ask Mona when she gets more pills. She needs to pay her for her silence either way. Really wishing she had a pain pill right now, she wonders, what's taking so long? They were only coming in for their statements, and now she's concerned if she's not released soon, she may not be.

Then the door opens, but it's not Detective Young; it's a butch, attractive woman of too many races to identify which she is most. Her walk is masculine, but her features are feminine and soft.

"Hi, Pru, I'm Chief Starr," she says, ignoring the chair and sitting on the table.

Pru removes her legs from their elevated position to give the chief her perch, speculating that Chief Starr is in her fifties for her noticeable crow's feet.

"You own a gun?" the chief asks directly, and Pru is thankful she worded it that way, so not forced to lie.

"No," Pru says.

"Ever shot a gun?"

"My father took me shooting when I was a kid."

"I spoke to your boyfriend already," declares Chief Starr. "You make an interesting looking couple." Pru smiles, acting naively, while she tries to figure out what was really meant by that. Was she referring to their age difference? The chief stares into her eyes and infers, "Being with crater face is a lot better than being alone, huh?"

Pru's smile fades, realizing that the accusations have already started. She will not be able to flirt her way out of this one. She will have to give up the naive act and let this woman know there is more to her than a pretty face and what was once gorgeous legs.

She fires back, "So, appearance is important to *you*?"

"You don't think so?" Chief Starr doubles down.

Pru can see she is not asking for herself. She thinks Pru is shallow and is using Carney for his fame or money, or both.

"Life's important to me," Pru states with passion. And in case Starr has looked into her background, she adds, "Positive choices and second chances."

"Enjoying your new life? Willing to protect it at any cost?"

Here we go, she thinks as the passive-aggressive assertions start flowing. "Maybe at some cost, but not murder," Pru states honestly. "I mean, all relationships require a little bit of sacrifice to protect it, especially in the beginning. And that's why all of my incoming calls are blocked, except for Carney's."

Chief Starr looks surprised, enlightened to that bit of information, and jots it down in a small notebook she pulls from her back pocket. "Thank you." She puts her notebook away and confesses a truth of her own, "I heard your statement, and..." Pru's suddenly concerned that her sweet demeanor with the first detective is in strong contrast to how she is now. She'll have to show the chief a sweet side, too, to be consistent. Chief Starr continues, "I also read the statement from Danny O'Brien." She looks Pru dead in her eyes for a reaction, but Pru remains frozen, wondering how they got to Danny so fast. Or did Danny come in to give a statement to defuse any suspicion about himself? *A friend masquerading as an ally.*

Continuing, the chief says, "Sounds like you have a lot of secrets. I wonder, what would you do to keep them from coming out?"

Pru answers her directly, "As women, we are the best protectors. I can see why you'd think that. You know more than anyone in here how true that is. I'm sure it's what makes you so good at what you do. You wouldn't be Chief otherwise." Starr gives a look like she might be right. "But I have no secrets. My protective impulse is not in play here. I'm injured, pretty helpless actually, just working on my recovery."

Chief Starr smiles as Pru fell right into her hands.

"Just how you like it. Maybe you'd even drag out your injury to keep this nightingale syndrome from expiring?"

Pru wouldn't put that past herself. She knows what she is capable of, but as Carney said, they are the victims.

She taps into the pain of her recovery, the pain she hid from Carney, and tells the chief, "I took a real hit, had to learn how to walk again, just look at my medical records."

"Let everyone believe you're the victim here, but I know you could've made that shot from the patio. The angle of entry matches up. It's only a matter of time before we can prove it."

Pru locks her lips. The game doesn't end here. The chief just told her as much already. The only thing on trial here is the chief's personal opinion of her. Pru now knows, being friendly isn't going to cut it with this woman, neither will logic. She'll have to rope-a-dope her way through it, stay in it and give everything she's got until the chief has nothing left and then nail her with a right cross at the end.

Meanwhile, Carney has no patience and sticks his head outside the office and attempts to get the attention of Detective Young, who's reading a file at a nearby desk. An African American hipster, the size of a football player with Warby Parker glasses and a poorboy hat, turns his head.

"How long I gotta wait?" Carney asks.

"Not a minute more," Detective Young calls back as he gets up to join Carney in the chief's office with a folder in hand. "I was reading up on this girlfriend of yours, Ruby, Pru." Young leans against the closed door. "Did you know she was a bad little girl? Got kicked out of two public schools and spent a few months in juvi."

Carney silently breaks down this plainclothes detective, but there's nothing plain about him. He's somewhere in his thirties but looks like he's in his twenties. And despite his earthy, sensitive, yet expensive apparel, his form underneath is strong like a collegiate athlete. Carney imagines he was a smart kid with minimal street experience before he ascended through academics with scholarships. If Carney were writing him as a character, this guy would be so unaware of who he is that he would consistently misread his suspects.

"There's good and bad in each of us," Carney professes to squash any doubt that he might have any doubt himself.

"Ya, bet she got spanked a lot. Bet she still does," the detective smirks, looking speculatively at Carney, whose blood pressure just raised dramatically.

"You're a jealous guy, aren't you?" the detective jabs.

Carney never thought of himself before as a jealous guy, although his body is telling him otherwise, and it's taking every bit of strength for him not to swing a punch.

"Hey man," the detective laughs, "you look like you're gonna kill me right now."

Carney cools down the fire inside him, calling upon his techniques as an actor.

"I'm with you," the detective continues, "I get you. She's hot. Looks like a fun ride. But, you ever wonder why she's with you? I mean, the chick's not exactly cut from the same cloth or same decade."

Carney watches as the detective sits at the chief's desk and opens Pru's file. Now Carney knows he and Pru are on their own, the advantages of his father have faded, it's rare birds against the world.

"Your judgment's not my issue, man," Carney scoffs.

"Callin' it how I see it, man," fires back the detective. "You have a failed director, once touted as 'the next Robert Conlon' now teaching community college and living off his father's legacy, and here comes sex-on-wheels in the peak of her youth with a checkered past that's worlds away from yours. And your friend is murdered?"

Carney doesn't even stiffen up. It's actually refreshing for someone to say that to his face, although he's never appreciated the comparison to Robert Conlon. The only thing he ever liked about Robert was his son, who worked as a projectionist at IFC in Hollywood. He met him years ago when he was color timing his first film. Back when you carried your film around in tin canisters and dealt directly with the projectionist. They had a lot in common, famous Hollywood fathers and instant judgment from anyone who ever met them and knew who their fathers were.

Detective Young can see he's losing Carney's interest and steps back toward the door, saying, "Let me show you something."

He holds the door open for Carney and then leads him down the hallway, stopping at the door marked Interrogation Room. The hipster detective sticks his head inside, leaving Carney in the hallway wondering. Of course, Carney has no idea that Pru is in that room, and Pru has no idea that Carney is out in the hall, but she does sense something's going down between the two detectives as Detective Young gives a cocky thumbs-up signal before shutting the door. Pru looks at the mirrored glass and has a feeling it has something to do with who is behind it or who will be behind it. She wonders if it will be Carney.

Detective Young leads Carney into the darkened two-way mirrored booth that feels like a small screening room. The way Carney sees it, the screen is the two-way mirror, and the actors in the scene are Pru and Chief Starr, who are lit incorrectly with fluorescent lights, and their voices are projecting through two large speakers. The only difference, there's no production assistant to bring him popcorn and bottled water. Carney and Detective Young take a seat and watch the show.

Chief Starr stands to pace the room, forming her next question thoughtfully. "Why did your parents really flee to Italy?" Starr asks. "Was it because they couldn't bear the truth that their daughter's a killer?" Pru shakes her head while Starr keeps railing on, "Did you kill all three of your exes or only the last two? Because you're getting sloppy."

Carney can't believe what she's asking her and thinks maybe Pru should have more of a reaction. But Pru sits calmly, giving the chief room to speculate, and every so often, her eyes dart toward the two-way mirror thinking of Carney.

"Does Carney know you were under investigation for Kevin's death?" Now Pru knows for sure that Carney must be behind the mirror. The chief obviously wants Carney to know.

"Maybe he does, maybe he doesn't," Pru says matter-of-factly, looking directly into the glass at a presumed place where Carney might be watching from.

Her eye-line isn't far off from where Carney sits. He stares back at her, assuming that Kevin was one of her exes unless there's another death he doesn't know about. It was never his interest to collect their names. It would have made it all the more real if he did. The detective watches Carney closely for a reaction, so Carney forces a bored expression like this is all old news.

Chief Starr circles behind Pru, spewing, "Do you know that it was only under burden-of-proof that you're not locked up? Everyone was convinced that you did it, but they couldn't prove it. That's the only reason it was ruled a suicide."

"Great to know that my testimony means nothing," Pru says sarcastically.

Carney sees how easy it is for people not to believe her, imagining this happens to her a lot. He wonders if he's been living in the bubble of his father for too long. And if stuff like this happens all the time to regular people. People like Pru. He longs to be by her side and never doubt her again.

With all seriousness, Pru declares, "Despite what you or anyone else thinks, I'm no killer."

Chief Starr feigns agreement with a nod.

Pru realizes the chief will need a more thorough answer to be convinced. "Anyone could be. It's a choice like anything else," Pru states as fact, appealing to the chief's logical side, "but it is the aftermath that separates us from psychopaths. The lifeblood of humanity running through our veins prevents us from acting upon impulses. Impulses mostly contributed to men."

Starr looks intrigued, but even though she's in agreement, she can't help but acknowledge the strangeness of such an answer. "Study serial killers or something?"

"No. I read a couple books on psychology," Pru bites back. Then looking at the two-way mirror, she's reminded of who else she's performing for. She assumes Carney is putting some pieces together, but he doesn't know her third guy's story. She thinks this is where she'll tell him, and grateful the glass is between them, it makes it easier.

"You know, I loved each one of them," Pru confesses, "never wished any of them harm, not even in our hardest arguments." She takes a breath, still having the chief's attention. "Coincidence is not burden-of-proof. And a pattern of bad luck is just that." In touch with the pain of her past, her eyes start to well up. She rarely lets anyone see her like this. It is a part of her that she protects with a wall of ice, but she knows how crucial it is for her real self to be seen.

"We were arguing on that rooftop, more him than me. He was drunk to the point of no longer being himself and accusing me of wanting to be with another guy or being with another guy. In his drunk, muffled yelling, it was a little hard to understand. It wasn't the first time he made drunk accusations, but it was the first time I was having none of it. I turned around to go, and that's when he threw himself into the shabby wooden railing and fell those six stories to his death. It still doesn't make any sense, but neither did he. He wasn't in his right mind. I ran to his side, to what was left of his crumpled body on the concrete. It was the most awful sight you could ever imagine, and I just sat beside him. I don't know if I was screaming or crying, but I was doing something, and people came out from the bars, watching me wail until someone pulled me away from him," she says as if back in that time and place with the pain of the tragedy on her face. Carney watches like it's a closeup, seeing her broken self on the asphalt next to her boyfriend's crushed body. She takes a breath as a tear rolls silently down her cheek. Carney feels the weight of her pain, wishing for this show to be over. They are long past giving statements.

"And where were the witnesses who saw me crying over his dead body?" Pru asks rhetorically. "How dare anyone think I'm a killer." She wipes a tear from her cheek. "Sometimes, bad things happen to bad people. Bad things happen to good people. Maybe the hammer was meant for me on the motorcycle and, since we dodged it, it came down on Mark. There's no explanation for why this happened. Only God knows the math. I'm sure if you look deep enough in the right direction, you'll see it's not me." She wipes her face and regains composure instantly.

Carney's impressed with her strength and her willingness to go to such a vulnerable place. He told her to do so, and she listened. She took his direction like an A-list actor.

"She's good. Have an agent?" Detective Young mocks.

Chief Starr, meanwhile, takes offense to her performance. She leans over the table and whispers threateningly, "What you both have doesn't exist. It's not real. The sooner you realize that, the better off you'll be."

Carney doesn't even try to make out what the chief says. Pru has all of his attention. The chief leaves the room and comes around to Carney's side of the two-way mirror to speak to Detective Young in private, outside in the hallway. Now Carney and Pru are alone, only separated by glass. Pru gets up and slowly walks toward the mirror. Carney watches her like she's a fish in a fishbowl. She puts her hand up to the glass, and he reaches out and puts his hand to hers. He feels connected to her in a way he's never had with anyone before. Pru has a feeling he's there but wants to know for sure, so she puts her ear to the glass to listen. She can't hear anything at first, but he taps the glass with his finger, and she flinches, giggling a little, and looks into the mirror, mouthing the words: *I love you too.* Carney can't believe his luck and wants to wrap his arms around her. This screening room is starting to feel like imprisonment. As he watches her walk back to the table, he wonders what Penny would do under interrogation. He pulls out his phone and begins typing.

PENNY

Where are the witnesses who say it wasn't self-defense? Sometimes, bad things happen to bad people. Bad things happen to good people. There's no explanation for why this happened. Only God knows the math.

James looks to the Federales like he's in the position to make a deal.

JAMES FINNEGAN

Unless you know a good accountant?

Carney, coming back to reality, looks back at Pru sitting there helpless and worried. His protective nature ignites, and his patience wears thin, but he knows he can't just fly off the handle and get mad at the detectives. They might gauge it as a form of guilt. He decides he'll call his attorney to make sure everything's on the up and up, but just then, Chief Starr and Detective Young come back into the viewing room and start in on Carney.

"Just a follow-up question," Detective Young says. "Why do you think she was scared? You said when you entered the house, she was afraid."

"Someone was shot; does she need another reason?" Carney asks with frustration. But apparently, they do need another reason because they stare back at him blankly.

He makes himself believe that he's calm, so he acts like it and imagines what else could have made her scared if it weren't for Mark.

"There's been a lot of crime and homelessness on the boardwalk. Have you seen it out there lately?" Detective and Chief both look shocked that Carney would be asking that of them. Carney's tone is relaxed, affirming, "People are trying to survive with nothing. There's enough gloom in those dark corners to scare even the lightest of angels because no one's doing anything about it. *You're* not doing anything about it."

Detective Young gets offended. "Hold on now, there's a lot about this grifter that you don't know."

Starr jumps in, "Let me fill in the blanks." She takes the folder from Detective Young. "In Las Vegas, after her boyfriend dies mysteriously, she goes to live with a known gangster who they believe she was having an affair with." He listens reluctantly, and she continues, "In Waikiki, her boyfriend dies of natural causes, and she said she wasn't there on the dock or in his boat to save him. But a witness puts her on the boat at exactly the right time."

He looks at how Chief Starr tries to emphasize her point by squishing her face with discontent. The way amateur actors do when they haven't embodied the character. It's a lie. He doesn't buy any of this as real facts.

"The suicide," she continues. "No witnesses saw him fall, but according to the family, it was a toxic relationship, and they believe she pushed him off the building," Starr finishes. "So... you see."

Carney looks at Pru and sees her more clearly than he's ever seen her before, caged and judged in a glass box. While, for some reason, completely unjustified, he's on the outside looking in.

He's starting to understand how and why she is the way she is and admires her strength for enduring it as long as she has. Looking at Chief Starr and Detective Young, he sees them, sees what they're trying to do and how they are working the case. He's had enough. "I see," he says. "You have no motive and no evidence. Instead of opening your mind up to the truth, you people make a judgment and then build a case around that," Carney asserts and stands with a quiet-confidence he's only seen his father embody on screen. "If we're all judged by our past, we'd all have no future. Like the homeless out on the boardwalk." He clamps down even harder, "If you continue to come after us, I'm going to use all of my power to stop you." Starr looks pissed. "We came here with hopes that we could help, and you're treating us like suspects while my friend's murderer is out there in the streets."

Starr has nowhere to go. Carney's attorney is one of the best in L.A. All she can do now is wait for the evidence.

"I'm sorry you feel that way," Starr says.

Carney walks past both of them and lets himself out. Walking over to retrieve Pru, he's aware of his emotional state. Every bit of them is on trial now. He focuses on his breaths, slow, and his heart rate, steady, not racing, not anxious. He feels powerful and free, if only for a moment, and for the first time in his life. It's all because of Pru. He opens the door and waves her over. She couldn't be more relieved to get out of there.

He extends out his hand and says nothing. He doesn't need to; she can read his strength and takes his hand—

it's something they do. Then they walk together, steady and tall, free from their pasts, and see only their futures in each other. Throwing open the door of the precinct with fortitude, he guides her into the parking garage.

At his Nova, he stares satisfyingly into her eyes. She wants to tell him *I love you too,* and as if he saw the pitch before it's thrown, he tells her, "I saw you through the glass."

"I knew it," she says with a smile.

CHAPTER TWENTY EIGHT

In a quaint old diner, Pru and Carney sit across from each other in a small booth by the window, leaning over the retro dinette table, secretively, like two criminals. She notices a change in him. He looks both like he's spent a week at a spa and just came off of a roller coaster, his eyes full of exhilaration yet calm and relaxed.

"Man, that felt good. You were good," he tells her, his hand reaching across to hold hers. "That's not exactly how I saw that going down, but wow."

She uses her free hand to adjust the diner's paper placemat, releasing some nervous energy. Then raises a mug of coffee to her lips. But before she drinks, she expresses her concern by mocking it, "How's it feel to be with a wanted woman?"

He smiles, and for a moment, she thinks he may be proud. It's that part of him that seeks for the danger that she likes the least, but she knows it's the reason that brought them together. He would never have been attracted to her otherwise, maybe sexually, but nothing more.

"They're bluffing. I could tell," Carney tries to convince himself, "but don't worry. I'll figure out what to do."

She has every reason to worry. In fact, with so many reasons and so few options, all she can do is trust. She does, though, probably more so than with any other man she's loved before. Yet, it doesn't make her feel any more at ease. She's nervous and anxious with her love. As she waits for him to come up with a plan, she sips and stares into his eyes and allows the diner chatter to surround her like a comforting blanket.

Then it comes to him; his gut tells him it's the only solution. "We head for the hills," he declares.

She gasps, almost taking her coffee into her lungs by accident. "What?" she asks while clearing her throat.

"We go on the run."

She thinks he must be joking. "This isn't a movie," she laughs, but he looks dead serious. She tries to wake him from himself, saying, "Carney?"

"It's all out of our control," he states with philosophic-undertones.

"We'll look guilty," she reasons, but he's not concerned.

"Look, if they don't have anything on us, then we're just on vacation in Mexico. We have a place down there," he says like his family's still alive. "And if they do have enough on us," he reasons, "then we made a good bet. We cash in our chips and stay on the run. I can write from anywhere."

She hangs her head in thought. She can't even believe she's considering such a radical idea. He makes it sound reasonable, and it's certainly not safe at the beach house anymore, plus she does trust him. He's changed her in that way. Staring down at the crossword puzzle on the placemat, she's reminded that love is a game, little battles and victories, and a lifetime of war. Initially, between the couple, until they unite against the world, and it's that war she wants to win, the war against the world. She could put her foot down and demand to stay and fight. She could persuade him if she wanted to, but what would she be fighting for and fighting against?

"So this is something you need?" she asks, making sure.

"This is something we need," he insists. "I don't want to be looking at you through bars hoping for a future we may never see," he pleads. "I've never felt more alive than when I'm with you, and you would've never been in this situation if it wasn't for me. Come on, you have to *run* before you can fly."

What can she say?

"I'm all in, Romeo."

He smiles victoriously, and the hairs on the back of his neck stand up. His senses are awake. In his mind, he is excited to plan their escape, to show Pru the bungalow in Mexico, and make love to her outside under the lush green canopy. He squeezes her hand with excitement, just as two plates are put down in front of them. They look up to see their waitress.

"I chose our famous black cherry pie," the waitress says, sliding a whole cherry pie in between them with two forks. "It's to die for."

CHAPTER TWENTY NINE

Carney places a to-go box on the roof of his Nova and pulls out his keys to unlock the passenger door for Pru. Across the street, he sees Danny walking toward Hemingway's Cigar & Bar. Carney could simply yell out to him. There's a lot they could talk about. Carney could ask him what he said in his statement and why he didn't call. The realization also occurs to him that Danny could be a suspect too; if the detectives were looking in all directions. After all, Mark had something over him. That's motive, more motive than Pru has. However, he fears this will all come down to ballistics on the bullet, and their only saving grace is that his dad's gun is unknown. And if Carney were a man of poor-morals, he could have his attorney make an issue of Danny to release the pressure off of Pru, but his heart aches just thinking of that. So he watches as Danny goes inside Hemingway's, wishing him a fond farewell from his heart. He is happy his friend is free of Mark's grip and wishes him well.

It suddenly registers to Carney that this was a deciding moment for him, a moral-defining moment, like what Pru told him. He feels empowered as he opens the passenger door, and it occurs to him to ask her, "You want to drive?"

"You're serious?" she beams with anticipation.

"I trust you," he says and hands her the keys, and she almost skips around the backside of the car with a grin a mile wide. Grabbing the to-go box from the roof of the car, he drops into the shotgun seat. He already feels the constraints of life lift from him, and his worries slowly start to evaporate. He's ready to take the passenger side of life and write what he sees because he has found his leading lady, his companion, his partner-in-crime.

She settles nicely into his seat, placing her cane in the back and adjusting the mirrors in her favor. If this role of woman-on-the-run is the one he wants her to play, she's born for it. Her hand turns the ignition, and the engine rumbles to her satisfaction. She backs up slowly, feeling the Nova's size, coming within a foot of another bumper. She looks at him with a confidence that he finds stimulating, then she grips the four-speed firmly and puts it into drive. He releases a laugh as she expertly maneuvers forward down the road, giving it an extra punch when she gets onto Pacific Avenue.

He realizes that running means he is in it too, from head to toe, both playing the same hand now, and he has a sudden desire to fold his cards of old. Pulling out his phone, he opens his Instagram app, goes to his settings, deletes his account, does the same with his Facebook, and the same with Twitter. He rolls down the window to feel the wind on his face. The streets of his neighborhood roll by, and he is without a care... That is until they arrive at his garage door, and find a notice taped on the outside. She looks at him inquisitively, and he gets out to see what it is.

He rips the search and seizure warrant and paperwork from the door and motions for her to open the garage. She hits the opener on the visor, and the door rises. He guides her in. The garage looks like it's been ransacked, and Carney only imagines what the inside will look like as he holds the driver's side door for her to get out.

"What is it?" she asks.

"See for yourself," he says, handing her the paperwork.

She grunts with the same displeasure he's feeling and walks inside, reading the sheet.

"They took my gloves and some dirty clothes," she says.

"Thankfully, my computer was in the car," he acknowledges, for fear that they would have confiscated it. Then he'd be without his ability to type his screenplay on something other than his phone.

Inside, they look around at the mess. Books are tossed on the floor, and furniture is flipped on its side. Carney places a few pieces upright.

"It feels like we were robbed," she exclaims.

"They're trying to peck away at us," he says as he muddles through the mess toward his humidor. Not only is it open, but his cigars are all tossed, and some are even on the floor. Picking one up from the hardwood, he cuts it and sticks it into his mouth, lighting it just right.

She walks over by the patio door to see if Mona is out there. At this point, she doesn't even care if Carney sees her buying black-market pills; they are potentially about to become fugitives from the law. But looking out the window, Mona's blue tent is gone, and Pru's concerned for her. Maybe Mona saw something, like Mark coming through the slider, and the police took her into holding for being a witness—she doesn't know what the policy is on that. Then she rationalizes it's possible that Mona just relocated because someone was killed where she slept and assumes she's just fine.

Pru gives in to her new reality. On the plus side, it will be easy to get what she needs in Mexico. There are no prescriptions required at *la Farmacia.* She sprawls onto the couch, without a care except for Carney. Her eyes locked onto him, waiting for her next cue.

He takes a seat on top of the table, seeing how sexy and dangerous she looks like she did when they first met. He could never have imagined this is where they'd be, but if he had to do it all over again, he would.

He asks, "I'm not afraid. Are you?"

"I've never known the word."

"Of course you haven't," he laughs.

"You know, you could've just walked," she declares, in a moment of seriousness for the decision they are making.

He shakes his head. "Where's the excitement in that?"

That's right, Pru reminds herself. His perception of her is exactly what he needs right now, to be wild and on the run. She gets back into character, playing the part. "The less we take, the better," she states, and he nods in agreement.

"We'll need some cash. Cash is king in Mexico," he says.

Taking a hit of his cigar, he recalls how his mom and dad set up a safe deposit box at First National Bank, in the case he was held for ransom and swept away by dangerous kidnappers. His parents kept adding to it every year up to his eighteenth birthday. He realizes now he never counted it and thinks it's ironic that his ransom money is what's finally setting him free. He saunters over to Pru on the couch, leans in close to her, thinking it must be pretty big, big enough to live on in Mexico. She runs her hands through his pompadour, wondering what he could be thinking.

"My dad left a lot of money in a safe deposit box for a rainy day," he tells her, remembering "for a rainy day" was the keyword to get the money.

She purrs like he knew she would. "Let's pack up this show, and get on the road, Romeo."

CHAPTER THIRTY

Completely exhausted, Carney slides out a large safe deposit box, heavily weighted, and sets it on the island in the middle of the vault. He opens the box, and there it is, resting on stacks of money that's deep and wide in the tray, his father's shiny gold Oscar.

He feels as if he just exhumed a piece of his father's soul. He stands the statue upright on the island, and for a moment, it's like his dad is there with him. As he looks back at the stacks of money, he can't forget the original purpose of it. He tries to imagine his mom or dad coming here to retrieve it to pay off his kidnappers and wonders, *is this how much I'm worth?* He feels the depth of his question as he packs all the money into his duffel, his father's Oscar staring at him the whole time. When he goes to put the Oscar back into the cold, metal box, something feels wrong. Looking at the gold figurine laying on its back in a silver box, reminds him of burying his dad all over again. So he decides to free him, too. Not knowing that he has other reasons for wanting to take the statue with him, his morals could break at any moment because the pillars that kept him inline aren't standing for him anymore. Subconsciously, Carney needs the reminder of his father to keep him toeing the line.

Dragging the heavy, wheeled duffle bag with the Oscar inside, he walks around the bank's facade to the parking lot. His dad's black trench coat whips in the air behind him as it did in *Walking Alone.* Knowing how suspicious he looks, he tries to be as unnoticeable as possible, limiting his movements to a slow, relaxed pace toward the running Nova. Spotting a silver car on the street with two men in it, facing his direction, he acts like he's doing nothing wrong, as mundane as picking up laundry. He opens the passenger side door and inconspicuously removes the figurine, handing it to Pru.

"Hold this for a sec."

"Holy shit," Pru says griping the statue as Carney lifts the duffle into the back.

"Heavy, right?" he responds, settling down in the shotgun seat, then strapping his seatbelt.

She takes a deep look at his father's prize, feeling the weight of its meaning as if she's meeting the father of the man she loves for the first time.

Carney briefly looks back at the two men in the silver car. The driver is staring at a large paper, like a newspaper or a map, and the other, well, he just turned his head to look in their direction.

"I think we're being followed," Carney says with a calm, serious tone. "Can you lose them?"

She hands him back the statue and revs the engine to signify she'll try, but she doesn't speed out of the parking lot as he imagined she would. Instead, she drives slow, pulling out through the side exit and makes a right, going past the silver Ford sedan with the two men. Carney keeps his head looking forward while his eyes look into the side mirror seeing the silver Ford pulling out to follow. She glides the car to stop at a stoplight a half a block up and looks in the rearview, seeing what Carney sees.

"They're following us."

"Yep."

Other than opponents on a drag slip, she's never tried to outdrive anyone before. Beyond that, there is another issue. How does she lose them without breaking too many laws? The last thing they want is helicopters chasing them to Mexico, and that's not even their first stop.

The light turns green, and she steps firmly on the pedal to push the Nova to the max allowed, which is 35 mph. She plans to get as many cars between them and the Ford. If she could just get around this teal Acura, but the driver's not letting her around. She puts on her blinker, threatening to come over anyway, and the Acura slows reluctantly down, enough for her to change lanes. Only now, she has an irritating tailgater. Carney watches Pru tensely, and not because he's nervous about her driving but because his PTSD is creeping up inside him and overriding his imagination to a horrific level.

Lincoln Boulevard is coming up. She can save a lot of time getting around the 405 freeway by taking Lincoln to the 105. She doesn't want to put her blinker on too early to give them a warning, so she waits to the last minute, blinker, and turn, pushing the Nova to 40 mph. She gets around another car, but that car turns right. Then here comes the Ford making the turn.

Thinking, it's possible these cops could think they are fleeing to the airport. She can use that to her advantage by staying in the right lane, the LAX turn-off lane. But as the traffic builds up, she quickly changes into the left lane avoiding the airport, and gets a whole five or six cars between them now.

Carney finds it helps to look at her instead of the road and feels especially at ease to see her smile. She takes the exit for 105 East and gets a huge break, all the slower cars are on the right, and she zips past all of them, getting a few more cars ahead.

When she looks into the rearview before changing lanes, the Ford is now only three cars back. She guns it up to 60 mph. *Only an asshole would pull me over for five mph over.* But she's still got them on her tail. If she doesn't lose them now, she might not be able to lose them on the 405. Meanwhile, the adrenaline keeps Carney awake.

Pru estimates it's a quarter-mile before the exit and sees a semi-truck ahead, tailed by an oil tanker. If she could time it right, she could get in front of them before the turn-off, and these guys won't know where they went. Staying in the far left lane, passing slower cars as she comes to them, she's not counting how many cars she has passed by, but it feels like four. She doesn't have time to look back and see where they are with the kind of maneuvering she's doing. The Nova's body language should tell them she's taking the 105 East for a long while, so she waits until she has a clear shot across the three lanes and goes for it, zipping ahead to get in front of the semi. She knows she's breaking a couple of traffic laws, no more than any Southern Californian asshole in traffic. It's not criminal yet.

She holds tight on the turn, still going 60 mph, and then speeds up to 70 mph when she merges onto the 405. Surprisingly, it's not that full, so she can needle in and out of cars smoothly without going too far over the speed limit. She dips into 75 mph at times. It's so easy to do. Her foot wants to floor it, but she restrains herself. Carney looks back to see where the Ford is. He can't find them, not at all.

"You lost 'em," he says, with a thrill in his voice.

She smiles, looking at him when she can. "I usually do," she says, realizing if there's something she's good at, it's losing men and fleeing the scene.

As the sun gets closer to its ocean dive, he enjoys the beautiful orange glow that paints her skin like a dye. He's in love with her, and he can't stop gawking. He likes her in charge. Her raven hair, pulsing in the wind from the open quarter winder as she pushes on, trying to get more miles between them and the Ford, he feels his luck changing, their luck changing, together.

CHAPTER THIRTY ONE

Hops stands in the driveway outside his single-story California ranch-style house, waving them toward one of the three garages that hook around the side of his Rolling Hills property. She carefully glides the Nova inside the open slot and kills the ignition, feeling proud of her driving skills.

"You're badass, babe," Carney says, then pops out of the passenger door with the Oscar and the duffle bag of money while Hops closes the garage.

"You look terrible," his godfather tells him. And after seeing the Oscar, he asks, "Have you been speaking to ghosts?"

"Maybe," Carney replies and gives him a hug. Then hands off the duffle bag with tired eyes. "We'll need to hide this from the *Federales*."

"He needs sleep," Pru warns.

Hops asks her, "What do *you* need?"

Upon further inspection, she's never much known what she needs. Shelter, food, and love seem like basic needs, but which shelter? What food? Who to love? She's been grappling with those questions for years, a result of her parents' early departure. Taking what comes her way, her method. That, and listening to her cardinal desires. Right now, she desires Carney, for all the right reasons. She grabs her bag from the trunk, but Carney quickly takes it from her and goes toward the door to the house. She follows behind him with her cane, entering before Hops and the duffle bag of money.

She feels comforted immediately by the cozy feel and amazed by all the cow-themed decor. The black and white patchy print is everywhere she looks. In the kitchen, it's a cookie jar, a soap dispenser, a towel holder. In the living room, it's a candle, a clock, a blanket, a rug, and even a cow-shaped ottoman. While she looks around with delightful intrigue, discovering more cows and cow print, Carney puts their bags down in the hall. Then plops down on the La-Z-Boy recliner, placing the gold statue on the couch beside him.

Hops cracks open a couple beers and hands one to her. "My Betsy collected all that," Hops says before delivering the other beer to Carney. "Made me nuts for a while. People kept bringing her more cow things, salt and pepper shakers, and potholders. I have a whole bag of cow print kitchen towels in the garage."

Pru laughs.

"But I miss it now," Hops confesses. "Sometimes I just buy something because I'm thinking of my Betsy."

"My mom collected spoons."

Hops is intrigued. "Oh, yeah? From different states?"

"No, different restaurants," Pru clarifies. But Hops can't make any sense of that.

Looking at a picture of Betsy and Hops in a cow print frame, she wishes she could've met her. With her fire red curly hair and hot pink nails, she looks like she was quintessential life, exuberant and delightful.

"What happened to her?" Pru asks.

He doesn't want to talk about cancer and the chemo, the pills and doctor appointments, and the vomiting and pain. He wants to remember her when she was healthy, and her spirit was unbreakable. "Love what you've got while you have it," Hops advises with his eyes welling up. "You never know how long God will grace you with it."

She squeezes his hand with empathy. "Isn't that the truth," she agrees, thinking of her long history with death. Then she looks to Carney, who's passed out on the recliner with his beer between his legs, and points it out to Hops in a silly way to uplift his mood.

He smiles, takes the beer from between Carney's legs, and puts the Oscar on the side table. He's relieved to see him sleeping, knowing his troubles with that. Pru lovingly covers Carney with a cow print blanket. And after Hops puts Carney's beer into the sink, he waves her over to the back door.

"Come with me," he whispers.

They leave the main house quietly and walk along the back porch toward a trail on the property. She's in awe of how breathtakingly beautiful it is here. The natural landscaping of sagebrush, yellow brush sunflowers, and California poppies gives her the sense that all is how it should be in the world. Nature has that power over her.

While he worries he might be walking too fast for her, he asks, "How's the leg?"

"Getting stronger every day," she declares, hearing a waterfall, like from an outdoor fountain, but can't locate where it's coming from.

"You're one tough cookie. I'll give you that."

She nods, accepting his compliment. She may not think of herself too highly in other areas, but she knows she's tough. She reckons he's fairly-tough himself, and seeing the mileage on his face, she can only imagine the things he's seen in his life. The death of his wife and his friend, the most obvious.

Hops adds, "Carney's no spring chicken, either."

"I know," she says, thinking of his unusual childhood. "He told me what he went through with the kidnap training."

Hops looks surprised, realizing now that she and Carney's relationship is more intense than he might have previously perceived. "He must really trust you," he assesses.

"He does," she beams. "Although, it isn't too hard to get Carney's trust."

"That's true." Hops laughs. "But as far as I know, he's never told that to anyone before."

"He loves me," she shares with a smile.

"Is that what you're in it for, the love? Or is there something else you're hoping to get from this?" Hops inquires, and she's not surprised. He has the right to be concerned about his godson. The optics from outside are what they are. The chief of police made that very clear. Perhaps one day, when her past is far behind her, she won't have to defend herself from inaccurate perceptions, but for now, she must.

"All I've ever wanted is for life to have meaning," she says, realizing, "Carney gives me that. And a purpose to my past."

"That's nice to hear," Hops says sincerely, feeling more at ease to discuss the past. "If he trusts you, then so do I. He had a rough go at growing up. Privileges, yeah, but mental unrest. Let me tell ya, the death threats were awful."

She listens.

"Carney, the poor kid, his mind wasn't quite right after that," he tells her with a sorrowful tone.

"It explains a lot, the earthquake box and fire extinguishers," she says.

"It's more than that," he says, admitting to himself that he might have to tell her something he's never told a living soul, other than Betsy.

She senses his seriousness.

He walks slower and explains, "When Carney was twelve, his parents were going through a divorce. He was being bounced back and forth like a pawn, and his father's womanizing created a psychopathic stalker."

She cuts him off, "Carney told me this morning."

"He did? What did he tell you?"

"His dad shot and killed her as she was breaking in."

"Hmm," Hops groans as he leads her toward a large, shed-like structure farther back on the ranch. "No," he continues, "it was Carney who shot her. And we swept it under the rug for the sake of the entire McMorris family." She's shocked but keeps her feet moving until her brain can catch up.

She knows there must be a reason why he didn't tell her. He could be ashamed or just in the habit of hiding it that he's convinced himself he didn't do it. How can he look to her like she's dangerous and exotic when he is the one who has done something like that?

As she and Hops approach the large shed, the sound of the fountain gets louder, and she wonders, "Why are you telling me this? Where are we going?"

He stops before the door, leaning on it with his palm. "Look, kid, before we go in here, I have to tell you something."

She feels anxious as he leans in close to her, and she wonders if she's worth more dead than alive. After all, everyone thinks she did it. If she disappeared, it would solidify her guilt to the cops. She watches him closely, aware of his hands.

He tells her, "I know you didn't do it, and I know you're standing by his side even though he's weaving it around in his head like a yarn that you did."

He grabs her hand, making her flinch, and pulls her reluctant fingers open to give her a heaping pile of rubber bands from his pocket. She looks at him confused, still trying to understand what's going on.

Then he opens the door to a large fountain, a three-tiered concrete deal like something from a western town. Beyond the large fountain are two beautiful brown quarter horses that fuss around in their stalls. She quickly puts together that this is his stable, and the rubber bands are to braid the horses' manes. She takes a breath and lets the mystery novel unwind in her head.

"That's Molly, and that's Pistachio," he says, pointing.

"They're beautiful," she says, navigating toward Molly, admiring her beauty.

Between the sound of the fountain and the horses' calming nature, she's becoming more relaxed, but she still has questions and more questions for her questions. Can the truth ever be known? What is truth? Does this change who Carney is or has been? Then she thinks about it in reverse. Should information about her past change how Carney should see her? She pets Molly on the nose and prays for certainty.

Hops watches her locate the dandy brush on the wall and begin to brush Molly's mane. He hopes this will be of comfort for her, so he opens the door to leave her to it.

"Hops?" she calls out to him before he goes through the door.

"Yeah?" He comes back in.

"Do you think Carney killed Mark?"

He stands there looking as troubled as she feels. "Who knows?" he admits and looks her dead in the eye. "Would it matter to you if he did?"

She looks into Molly's big beautiful black eye for the answer, but all she sees is her conflicted face reflected back.

Hops pats her on the back before leaving her with her thoughts. She brushes and braids, remembering the little girl she used to be, so hopeful, optimistic, trusting, and how the world made her jaded and cynical. She neither regrets nor is remiss for her past. It made her strong and all the things Carney needs. She moves on to Pistachio until time blends and bleeds.

She can't even remember how or when the lights came on. Petting Pistachio and Molly goodbye, she slowly walks back up to the house. Her leg is sore from standing for so long, but she makes it back to the house without falling on the path. The living room is quiet. The Oscar looks out over a crumpled cow print blanket on the couch and no Carney. She hobbles down the hall to find him asleep in a guest room, decorated the only way she'd expect, cow prints everywhere, and her bag is on the floor by her side of the bed.

Sitting on the edge the bed, she looks at him sleeping. Reminding herself of what she knows because it's hard for her to imagine him killing someone, and she wonders if this could happen again. Could he ever point the gun at her?

After brushing her teeth and changing into Carney's Cryptid Animals t-shirt and a pair of his boxers, her new favorite pajamas, she tries to imagine her life without him. Where would she go? She imagines driving her beaten-down car through the streets, looking up old acquaintances for a place to stay. Since Doug is entirely out of the question now, she'd have to knock on some doors that have previously closed. Hoping her injury garners her some added sympathy.

She doesn't know what she could do for money. Even if she got a job, it would have to be one without long hours of standing or walking. She imagines being miserable with that routine. It wouldn't be long before loneliness would override her motor functions and all her mechanics go haywire. She'd be at a nightclub looking for someone that could never be Carney.

She slides into the bed next to him and watches his chest rise and fall with each breath. She reminds herself again that he shot a woman, but then also reasons that he was frightened, especially being so young. It was self-defense, a terribly traumatic event, and she could understand. She wonders if he really believes that his father pulled the trigger? We all tell ourselves lies to get us through, she admits, and wonders what hers might be. Does she put too much into the idea that bad luck is responsible for her shortcomings and doesn't hold herself accountable? If she were never with Kevin, would he have jumped or fallen from the roof? She has to admit, for someone who doesn't like to lie to other people, she does a whole lot of lying to herself. If she would have opened her eyes, she could've easily seen how wrong she and Kevin were for each other. She could have done the right thing before he did the wrong thing.

She tosses and turns, worried she'll wake Carney with each movement, making it impossible to sleep. Even when she does manage to get a little shut-eye, she has that reoccurring dream again. She's falling off a cliff, digging her nails into the dirt, then falls and wakes up before she hits the ground. Up with her thoughts again. She wonders if Carney is capable of shooting Mark. She never really thought of it as a possibility before, but now she can't get it out of her mind. He'd have to have another gun, and as far as she knows, he doesn't.

She replays that tragic night over and over again. She aimed the gun at Mark, but he was gone. Only the open front door stared back at her, so she closed it and was going to sweep the house, in case he opened the door as a diversion, but first, she had to close the sliding door, so he couldn't come back in again. That's when the shots were fired. She was almost to the slider when she heard it, two of them, back to back. It sounded so loud. A few minutes later, when she didn't hear anything, she looked through the slider and saw Mark lying flat on the concrete boardwalk. If he weren't wearing his loud pattern jacket, she wouldn't have known it was him. It was a dark night, too dark to see if anyone was hiding in the shadows.

Imagining a scenario where Carney did it, she figures he left the house with the other gun, which would have been hidden in the bedroom, somewhere she hadn't snooped. Did he leave the house but stay close by? No. He would have seen Mark come in, and he would have done something, she answers herself. So he left for a walk and came back, seeing Mark run from the house, and did it then.

In this hypothetical scenario, she wonders how she'd feel if she were to be arrested instead of him. Innocent people are sent to prison all the time, and if she's honest with herself, she feels like she might actually deserve the punishment. In no way has she been useful to society. She's not a taxpayer or contributor. She's a taker, and her sticky fingers have stolen a few cookies over the years. So she could live with that judgment if she had to.

She stares up at the ceiling and imagines being locked away in a cell. *What would time feel like?* But she falls asleep and has the same dream again. This time, time moves slower, and she manages to grab ahold of the rock jutting out from the cliff. She did it, changed her dream, she realizes, while still in it. Then the rock dislodges, and she falls again. Only instead of face first, she has her back to the ground. She tries to maneuver her body to turn around and flips over in a flying position. She is flying! Gliding over the beach and along the coastline, over the houses and down low, landing on a tree branch. Then she wakes up again, thinking that was amazing, wishing she could fall asleep again so she could fly, but sleep is not coming.

Morning is coming, though, and she is nowhere near deciding how she feels. Morally, if she were to know that he killed Mark, would standing by him mean that she's okay with murder? Will she find out later that Carney is a violent menace and may shoot her during a fight? Are the unknowns enough to keep her from his love? Is her love blind?

The glow of a giant digital alarm clock reads 5:10AM. She figures it's morning enough and quietly goes into the kitchen to make coffee. A cow print coffee container with filters inside stands next to the coffee maker. Easy enough. She opens the cabinet for a mug and sees a picture of 15-year-old Carney with Hops and Betsy taped on the inside cabinet door. His cystic acne litters his face and neck, red and swollen spots so clustered and vast that he looks infected. She touches the photo, feeling for his painful years. Especially being the son of such an iconic public figure, he had to feel like a curse to his family.

Selecting a cow mug with utters for the base, she waits for the coffee to brew and looks out the window to see two ravens on the fence. By their size, she assumes they've been together a long time. The way they communicate with each other, so playful and connected, like how she feels with Carney.

She pours herself a cup before it's finished brewing and cuddles up on the couch with the cow print blanket. Looking around Hops' living room with the Oscar staring at her, she sees the movie posters from the films he was in with Mitch and framed pictures of them on set and tries to imagine Carney's life being surrounded by all of this. Adding into that the kidnap training and a psycho stalker, everything in his life is so dramatic. She would think he'd long for a steady calm like her.

Looking at the floor, she sees Carney's duffle bag. Setting her coffee on the side table beside the Oscar, she goes to the duffle, zipping it open to see the money. So many stacks of crisp twenty-dollar bills. She's never seen that much money before. She picks up one of the stacks and flips through it, thinking she could call a cab and go anywhere she wants. She would find a way to live the rest of her life on that money. She could keep a low profile and live off the grid. There's a lot of money there. Although there is that silly issue of murder hanging over her head, so she doesn't imagine she'd get very far. Then there is Carney. She would miss him. He would let her go if that was what she wanted. He could make sense of it, but it would be a wound too deep to repair. She would have to live with that guilt, all the while wondering if it were even necessary. There is a chance that Carney is not Mark's killer and may never kill again. She looks one more time at the duffle of money before zipping it shut.

At some point, she wonders if Carney's looseness with the truth will be an issue. Especially the lie she's living with him right now. The lie that she's a killer. What would happen if she forced the truth into their relationship? Would they crumble? Or does he need this fantasy? She locates a pen and paper over by the landline phone and cuddles back on the couch, putting pen to page in the only way she knows how to work out her feelings.

Weaving the fantasy of his choosing,
Do we flee?
Once I was cryptid,
But will he ever see?
The blackness in my wings,
The sharpness of my beak?

Will truth ever be what he seeks?
Or am I the mythical animal,
tossed aside when his story ends?
What do I decide?

Before she knows it, the daylight is creeping in, and she hears footsteps down the hall.

"Morning, Angel," Hops says, cheerfully, in his red plaid robe and matching slippers.

"Morning," she mutters.

"Sleep well?"

"I made coffee," she dodges the question.

"Like I said, an angel."

He pours a cup and sits near her in the recliner, and addresses the day. "When Carney gets up, he and I are going to stack the money in the car door."

"I'll hop in the shower then," she says and puts her mug in the sink, looking for the ravens out the window, but they're gone.

Back in the guest room, Carney's still asleep. She gets fresh clothes from her bag and crosses the hall to the bathroom. Her unfinished poem rattling around in her head:

Weaving the fantasy of his choosing,
We flee.
Once I was cryptid,
But will he ever see?
The blackness in my wings,
The sharpness of my beak?
Will truth ever be what he seeks?
Or am I the mythical animal,
tossed aside when his story ends?
What do I decide?

In the shower, she tries not to get her hair wet. She doesn't have a blow dryer, and she doesn't want to go to jail with damp hair because she's concerned they will open the garage to find a slew of cop cars out there waiting to nab them or her. What's strange is that she used to love the unknown and the bountiful possibilities it possessed. It excited her, and now all it does is shake her at her core. Maybe because she finally has something she doesn't want to lose. Is that the answer she is looking for? If it is, then why does she still have this desire to flee? She needs to talk to Carney.

She dries, dresses, and throws her hair back in a ponytail. She expects to find him still in the guest bed, but he's not there. She packs up her bag and goes to the living room. No one's there, and neither is the duffle of money. She walks out to the garage with her cane and overnight bag only to find Hops inserting money into the inner door panel of Carney's Nova.

"Can you hand me the Phillips?" Hops asks her with his hands busy holding it together. She hands him the Phillips screwdriver, and he's delighted she knows what it is.

"Where's Carney?" she asks.

"He wanted to feed the horses. Hold this," he instructs.

She assists, allowing herself to get dragged into helping him fill both door panels and the extra stacks he sticks in the dashboard behind the stereo. Afterward, he hands the screwdriver to her.

"You trust *me* with the key?" she asks.

"You're the handy one in the family now."

She basks in the warmth of being considered part of a family. Having felt like an orphan for so long now, she wonders if it's the assurance she needs.

When will I know?
Will I always just go with the flow?

Popping the trunk, she places her bag inside, but she can't slide it in far enough. It keeps catching on something. Moving it in another way, she hears the tearing of velcro and investigates. Under the carpet, there is a hidden compartment. She looks to see if Hops is watching, but he's just cleaning up the garage, so she pulls back more of the velcro carpeting and sees a secret compartment. Opening it, she sees a gun, not the Colt. It's a black 9mm handgun.

She realizes this could be the gun Carney used to kill Mark. In fact, she's sure of it now. But before her thoughts can process this, Carney comes into the garage with his bag, so she closes the compartment, fixing the velcro, and puts her bag over it.

"Ready to roll," Carney exclaims enthusiastically. His hair is wet from what must have been a quick shower.

Her eyes are transfixed upon him as if she is meeting him for the first time and trying to size him up. All this time, she thought she was the cat. But she's never felt more like a mouse caught in a trap. Coming over to her, he puts his bag in the trunk beside hers. He smells clean like Irish Spring, but soap can't wash away what's happened. Their hands are dirty, and they are in this together.

"Good morning, beautiful," he says, leaning in for a kiss.

Inside she wants to rebuild her walls, but his kiss is tearing every brick down. His lips are warm and comforting, like a blanket by the fire on a cold winter night. Her heart of hearts tells her he is a good man, and even though he killed Mark, he will never hurt her. He was protecting her. She melts into his embrace. She now knows he's the one she's been searching for, dreaming for, her flawed hero come to life. He may live in a fantasy of his choosing, but she lives in a reality without choice. They are misunderstood misfits who have endured tremendous trauma, and she has faith that together, they can heal the other's wounds. She thinks:

> I decide.
> Heart kissed, truth unknown, I decide.

And looking at him with loving eyes, she asks, "Sleep well?"

"Like a baby," Carney replies, then pats her on the butt to put her into gear.

She hugs Hops and goes around to the passenger side, for she is in no condition to drive today. Coffee and anxiety are keeping her awake. As she gets into the Nova, she thinks any moment, the door will open, and it won't matter that she has decided. Or that she knows Carney is a good man, and together they can be redeemed. The door will open, and there will be cops. She nervously watches as Hops opens the garage door while Carney adjusts his mirrors and fires up the engine. Her heart thumps in her chest.

Carney rolls down his window and tells Hops, "I'm going to send you a ton of script pages, be ready to read."

Pru stares into the side mirror, waiting for the door to fully open and reveal what's out there. So far, it's all gravel, more gravel. That's it, gravel. No cops. She takes a deep breath.

Hops waves goodbye.

As they cruise down the hill, she wonders if this is what paroles feel like, free but not free, like the door could slam on them at any moment. She looks out for cars that could be following them, but they're in the clear. It can't be, she tells herself, and rolls down the window for air. She worries that they could have a follow car trail off and be replaced by another follow car. She wishes she could just relax.

Getting on the freeway, he merges and changes lanes. The highway is wide open, so he punches the gas flying into the fast lane. It's like a wind tunnel with the windows down. Her ponytail is whipping around behind her head, and all she hears are the whips of the wind. She laughs, giving in to the madness, and puts her hand out the window, feeling the wind in her palm and her poem in her head.

I decide. Love.
My truth unknown, I still decide.

Everyone weaves a story,
Not always weaved in glory,
There are no heroes,
Or villainous crows.
We can all fly from the nest,
To become our best.
You played my game and twisted the tables,

How could I ever decide I'd rather go back to the stables?

They lock eyes for a moment and share a quick smile. Then he puts his hand out the window like her, and she realizes from outside their arms could look like wings.

And as they soar downward toward the fantasy of their choosing, a notification comes up on Carney's phone that goes unnoticed. "LA TIMES NOTIFICATION A second bystander shot on Venice Beach boardwalk as homelessness rises."

So flee,
All in, And we'll see.
Luck or loss,
Our lives intercross.
Insane or in pain?
We're just ravens in the rain.

THE END

Dedicated to
LOVE, and optimistic gamblers of the heart.

ABOUT AUTHORS

Jeff & Christie Santo have been married for over 10-years. Christie has her Bachelor of Arts degree in creative writing from California State University Long Beach. Jeff has over 25-years of filmmaking experience, directing and writing, with memberships in both the Writer's Guild of America and Director's Guild of America. And this is their first novel together.